"Whattaya say, partner? Wanna go make nice?"

He glanced down at Boyd. His canine buddy was stretched out in a patch of late-morning sunlight.

Groveling really shouldn't be all that tough for him, but because she was brighter than most, she'd see right through his usual I'm-just-a-guy approach. That meant he'd have to go with the truth.

Hoping to appear contrite, he shoved his hands in the pockets of his jeans and trudged down the steps. In the yard, he intercepted Chelsea.

"I'm sorry."

"For what?" she countered tartly. "Being you? Please."

"For being out of line. I hope you can forgive me."

The change in her was remarkable. He'd braced himself for a scolding, but what he got instead was a slowly dawning smile. By the time it reached her eyes, he glimpsed a sparkle in them he'd never seen before. How many guys had gotten that view of her? he wondered briefly before slamming the door on his curiosity. He had no intention of going anywhere remotely personal with her, so there was no point in even asking the question.

Books by Mia Ross

Love Inspired

Hometown Family
Circle of Family
A Gift of Family
A Place for Family
**Rocky Coast Romance*
**Jingle Bell Romance*
**Seaside Romance*
†*Blue Ridge Reunion*

*Holiday Harbor
†Barrett's Mill

MIA ROSS

loves great stories. She enjoys reading about fascinating people, long-ago times and exotic places. But only for a little while, because her reality is pretty sweet. Married to her college sweetheart, she's the proud mom of two amazing kids, whose schedules keep her hopping. Busy as she is, she can't imagine trading her life for anyone else's—and she has a pretty good imagination. You can visit her online at www.miaross.com.

Blue Ridge Reunion

Mia Ross

Recycling programs for this product may not exist in your area.

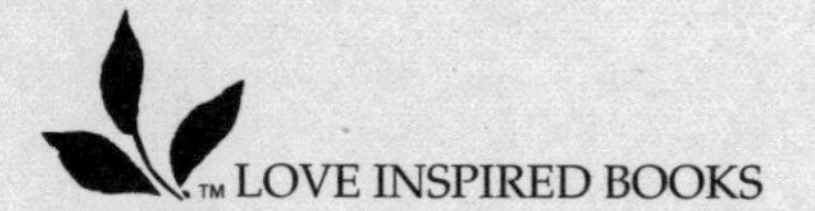

ISBN-13: 978-0-373-87904-5

BLUE RIDGE REUNION

This edition published by arrangement with Love Inspired Books.

www.Harlequin.com

Printed in U.S.A.

Let us not grow weary of doing good, for in due season we will reap, if we do not give up.

—*Galatians* 6:9

For Mom and Dad

Acknowledgments

To the very talented folks who help me make my books everything they can be: Elaine Spencer, Melissa Endlich and the dedicated staff at Love Inspired.

More thanks to the gang at Seekerville (www.seekerville.net), a great place to hang out with readers—and writers.

Thanks to RL for your insights into the banking world—and for the lunch.

Chapter One

Chelsea Barnes really hated Mondays.

Especially Mondays like this, when the July sunshine and warm breeze tempted her to stay home from work and enjoy the beautiful summer day. But her father had taught her that people who played hooky never amounted to anything, so she refocused on the narrow two-lane road. Following it as it meandered under the leafy canopy of oaks, she kept an eye out for the turnoff she needed. Around a bend, she located the weathered sign dangling from one rusty hook: Barrett's Sawmill, est. 1866.

She drove slowly down the pitted track, avoiding the largest ruts and hoping the pinging gravel didn't take too much paint off her darling convertible. At the other end, she pulled up alongside a beat-up red pickup with the sawmill's faded logo stenciled on the driver's door. It was so old she wouldn't be surprised to discover it had rolled off the assembly line when Henry Ford was still in charge.

Seeing it here was odd, she thought as she stepped from her car. While reading through the loan application file, she'd gotten the impression the property had been abandoned since the Barretts closed down their bankrupt company ten years ago. She surveyed the place with a glance but didn't notice anyone. What she did see was the millhouse, stubbornly clinging to the bank of the creek that once powered its waterwheel and looking every minute of its considerable age.

Deciding it was best to get this over with quickly, she shouted, "Hello? Is anyone here?"

Her greeting unleashed an unmistakable baying, and a huge red bloodhound came bounding from a nearby grove of trees, ears flapping as he made a beeline for Chelsea.

He wasn't snarling or showing his teeth, but she'd rather not find out the hard way that he wasn't friendly. Keeping her eyes fixed on him, she retreated to her car and fumbled behind her for the door handle.

Unable to locate it, she scrambled onto the hood. "Hello? A little help out here!"

No one appeared, but a commanding voice boomed from inside. "Boyd, that's enough!"

Instantly, he dropped to a sitting position, wagging his tail on the ground while his tongue lolled from his mouth in a sloppy welcome. Reassured, Chelsea eased herself to the ground and looked up to find the dog's owner strolling down the rickety porch steps toward the driveway. *No,* she groaned inwardly. She hadn't seen him in ages, but she instantly recognized that cocky walk, those long, powerful legs and impossibly broad shoulders.

Paul Barrett. Valedictorian, captain of any team he played on, dream date of every cheerleader at Barrett's Mill High School. In other words, the bane of her teenage existence.

What on earth was he doing here? Last she knew, he was in Kansas somewhere, doing whatever appealed to him at the time. It had never occurred to her that when her father had said his bank was doing a favor for the Barretts, Paul would be involved. Arrogant and unpredictable as a summer storm, here he was, smiling at her as though they were old friends. Which, of course, they weren't.

But standing here in front of the rustic building, surrounded by acres of trees, she grudgingly admitted he'd gotten better looking over the years. When he smiled, that opinion only deepened. Then he started talking.

"Chelsea Lynn Barnes," he drawled, his dark eyes crinkling as he squinted into the sun. "What's a classy girl like you doin' out here in the sticks?"

Just like that, her earlier annoyance returned, and she had to bite her tongue to keep back a sharp response. The fact that she'd been wondering the exact same thing had nothing whatsoever to do with her reaction. While her father had framed this trip as a personal favor to him, she couldn't quite shake the suspicion that she'd drawn this assignment for no reason other than that she was the only one on his staff who knew how to get to this map-dot town buried in Virginia's Blue Ridge mountains. Taking a calming breath, she reminded herself this was business and she had to maintain a professional demeanor. Even if it killed her.

Sliding a business card from the outside pocket of her slim briefcase, she replied, "I'm a commercial loan officer for Shenandoah Bank and Trust in Roanoke. I'm doing the property appraisal for the loan you requested."

Next time, she vowed silently, she'd read a prospective client's file more carefully. If she'd done that this morning, she could've braced herself to see Paul instead of getting blindsided like this.

He took the card and eyed her skeptically, then grinned. "What's the punch line?"

People frequently did this to her, assuming she was too young to handle so much responsibility. With anyone else, she'd have taken the slight in stride. But Paul had rubbed her the wrong way from the day they'd been tossed into the same kindergarten class, seeming to delight in pushing her buttons.

She pulled herself up to her full height and gave him her coolest look. "I assure you, I'm well qualified to make financial recommendations to the bank."

"*Daddy's* bank." Plunging grease-stained hands into the front pockets of jeans that had seen better days, he rocked back on the heels of his battered work boots. "How do you like working for him?"

No one had ever asked her that, probably because they assumed her current position was a cakewalk. Having known Theo Barnes all her life, she was better acquainted with his impossibly high standards than anyone. There were days when she wondered if she'd ever meet them, as either his daughter or his employee.

Shunting that grim thought aside, she said simply, "It's going well." Of course, her answer depended on which day you asked her. Today, for instance, she wasn't all that crazy about it, but there was no way she was sharing that with Paul.

He gave her a long, assessing look that told her absolutely nothing about what was going through his mind. Not that she cared on a personal level, of course. It would just be nice to know so she could plan her next move and keep ahead of him. That was the mistake she'd made all through high school, she'd realized over the years. She'd never had the upper hand, and he'd beaten her out of more awards—twelve, to be precise—than he should have.

While they stared at each other, the wind ruffled his unruly brown hair, and she couldn't help noticing the lighter streaks running through it. Judging by his tanned face, he still spent a lot of time outside, and he probably felt totally at home in these untamed acres of woods surrounding the mill. While she preferred well-groomed men with a sense of style, she couldn't deny that Paul had his own raw appeal.

For other women, she amended quickly, yanking her errant thoughts back from where they had no business going. "Are you the new owner of the property?"

"Yup."

He offered nothing more, and she decided that in the interest of preserving her sanity, it would be best to move things along. "Shall we get started outside?"

Humor twinkled in his eyes, joined by an aggravating smirk. "Yes, we shall."

She picked up on his mocking tone and did her best to ignore the dig as he motioned her ahead of him. An hour, tops, and she was out of here. Then she'd stamp his loan request *denied* in bright red ink. Maybe she'd do it more than once, just to make a point.

Her father's distinctive ringtone sounded in her bag, and she bit back a sigh before answering. "Hi, Dad. No, I didn't get lost. In fact, I'm standing in front of the mill now." She felt uncertainty beginning to creep in. She was twenty-seven, but having him check up on her this way made her feel ten again. "Of course. He's right here."

Something aggravatingly close to sympathy softened Paul's rugged features as he took the phone from her. "Good morning, Theo. What can I do for you?" He listened, then replied, "This arrangement works fine for me. I've got no doubt Chelsea can handle whatever needs doing."

The unexpected show of confidence meant a lot to her, and she mouthed, "Thank you."

Winking at her, he waited for her father to finish whatever he was saying. "My family and I appreciate you giving us a shot. Take care."

Thumbing the disconnect button, he handed the handset back to her. He didn't say anything while she muted it and returned it to her bag. Embarrassed by her father's call, she took out her camera and busied herself with the clasp on its case.

"So," Paul began in a tone edged with sarcasm. "Your father hasn't changed much."

He'd put her exact thought into words, and she was torn between agreeing and scolding him. When she caught the humor in his eyes, she said, "I guess not."

"Is he always that tough on you?"

"He's tough on everyone," she snapped. "I can't expect special treatment because I'm the boss's daughter."

Paul held up his hands as if to fend off her temper. "I didn't mean anything by it. It just surprises me that he doesn't have more faith in you, is all. You'd think he'd know better than anyone how smart you are."

She responded with a sharp, very unprofessional laugh. "Tell him that, would you?"

"Gimme your phone and I will."

Judging by his somber expression, he was deadly serious. Despite their old rivalry, she was touched by the gesture, and she rewarded him with the genuine smile she rarely used during business hours. "That's sweet of you, but I was only kidding."

Bit by bit, that maddening grin returned. "Be honest now. Back in high school, did you ever think someday you'd be saying I was sweet?"

"Not in a million years."

She admired how he'd shifted from kindness to teasing, clearly attempting to make her feel more at ease. As they smiled at each other, she recalled that he'd always had a way with people. Young, old, male, female, popular or not so much, it didn't matter. Back then she'd envied him that skill, and now she recognized that her envy had tainted her memories of him. Standing in the warm sunshine with him, she appreciated his generosity more than she could say.

Before she could blurt out something she'd probably regret, she recentered her mind on work. That strategy had worked well throughout her career, and she gladly retreated into it now. "I need to document the condition of the property for your application. What's first?"

While they toured the exterior, she began to worry there was nothing worth saving. The cobblestone bridge leading to the back entrance seemed fairly solid, but instinct warned her it would never pass a modern engineering inspection.

When she said as much, his answer surprised her. "Oh, that's all solid steel underneath, and only twelve years old. I had it inspected last week, and it's plenty strong enough for modern trucks to come in and out. The river rock's just cemented on for looks."

Impressed by his foresight, Chelsea made a note in the condition column. "I'll need a copy of that report."

"No problem."

The mill itself was post-and-beam construction, built of oak from the nearby forest. But the roof appeared to be suspect, and everywhere she looked, significant pieces of the structure were either sagging or missing completely. Alongside the damaged areas hung fresh boards, which stood out from the weathered siding like hopeful signs of improvement.

Once they'd finished their circuit, Paul turned to her with an expectant look. "Whattya think?"

"I think you need a bulldozer and some condos right over there."

When she pointed to the low hill overlooking Sterling Creek, for some reason he chuckled. "Not so fast. You haven't seen the inside yet."

She couldn't imagine it would make a bit of difference in her assessment, but out of fairness, she tamped down her impatience to get back to civilization. "All right. Let's have a look."

The boards on the wide stairs were weathered gray and rocked under her designer heels with each step. The handrail wasn't much help, but considering her odd reaction to seeing him again, she didn't want to get too close by steadying herself on Paul's shoulder. His dog rumbled past them, nearly knocking her down. When Paul reached out a hand to help her, she pulled out of range. "I'm fine, thank you."

"Stubborn as ever," he muttered, adding something she didn't quite catch. It was probably better that way.

The interior of the building was in slightly better shape, but not by much. On closer inspection, she noticed some of the belts on the antique equipment had been replaced, and the smell of oil and sawdust hung in the air. To the right of the door was what used to be a seating area. Now it was filled with a jumble of filthy equipment in various stages of repair.

On the other side was an office with a half door that stood open to the entryway. Inside she noticed a scarred but sturdy-looking table, a couple of mismatched chairs and an old settee covered in what she assumed was bloodhound fur. There wasn't a hint of a computer, which didn't surprise her in the least, but along the far wall stood a dusty row of filing cabinets that probably contained paperwork decades older than she was. In the corner near the window was a small woodstove that held an old boom box playing a mellow rock tune she recognized from high school dances.

When she spotted the air mattress and sleeping bag, she turned to Paul in amazement. "How long have you been living here?"

"About a month, off and on. I'm officially staying in town with my grandparents, but when I'm working late, Boyd and I crash here."

The million-dollar question, she thought, was why? Since they'd never see each other again after today, she decided to ask. "Your father shut this place down ten years ago. Why are you trying to bring it back now?"

His expression dimmed a little, even though the sun was still shining gamely through the grimy paned windows. After a moment, he answered. "It's for Granddad. He wants to see it up and running again, and that's reason enough for me."

The flicker of sadness in his eyes told her there was more to it than that, but she didn't want to pry. She remembered Will Barrett as a kindhearted man who'd inherited an archaic family business rooted in another century. When it failed, she hadn't been surprised, or even particularly sorry. But now she felt the very thing her father had warned her about before coming out here: sympathy.

In her memory, she heard him reminding her that sentiment had no place in the banking industry. She was here to do a job, not get wrapped up in someone else's family problems. The bank—and more precisely, her father—was counting on her honest, objective appraisal before approving or rejecting this loan request. More than anything, she wanted to prove to him that she was capable of taking over the helm when he was ready to step down. That was what he'd planned for her all her life, and as his only child, she was determined to make it happen.

That meant playing the game by his rules, which didn't include financing a business so far off the beaten path it couldn't help but fail again. In spite of her personal opinion, she was touched by Paul's willingness to take on a hopeless cause for his grandfather. Not for himself, or for money, but because Will had asked him to. Few people got through the composed demeanor she'd cultivated, but Paul's direct, heartfelt explanation had come uncomfortably close to doing just that. What that meant she couldn't say, but it was a disturbing feeling, and she fought it with every disciplined bone in her body.

"It looks like you've been making progress with the equipment." Some things looked completely worn-out, but others were clearly fresh out of the box. "Is this what you wanted to show me?"

"Yeah." Brightening, he strode past her to an old wooden lever. "I just finished this section, so I haven't tested it yet. You might wanna cover your ears."

Slinging her camera around her neck, she followed his suggestion. When she nodded that she was ready, Paul braced his hands on the lever and peered through a hole in the floor. Apparently satisfied, he gradually moved the handle from left to right, unleashing a metallic grinding noise.

"The door in the dam's opening," he explained loudly. "It lets water in from the creek to spin the wheel."

She nodded again, looking down as water rushed in and over the paddles in the newly repaired waterwheel. Once it was spinning, Paul moved away from the lever and pulled a wooden handle on the far wall. It released the mechanics of the main saw, sending belts over pulleys, back and forth, to drive the blade. The noise was deafening, but the motion was even more remarkable. Once the contraption was in full gear, the entire building shook with the power created by a modest stream and a bunch of leather belts.

She'd been here on tours in elementary school, but now Chelsea saw more than the interesting mechanics of days gone by. She admired the genius behind the original design and the skill required to bring all that creaky equipment back up to speed. While Paul had completed only one of the four saw channels, it didn't take much to envision the business in full operation, churning out lumber for furniture and flooring the way it once had.

After Paul powered everything down, she said, "This place used to be run by electricity. What made you decide to go back to waterpower?"

"Waterwheels are cool," he answered with a little boy's enthusiasm. "That's how it was when Granddad was a kid, so I wanted it to be that way again."

Again, she sensed there was more to tell, but she didn't want to get sucked into the charming picture he was painting for her, so she opted to keep things strictly professional. "I have to admit, you've accomplished a lot in only a month."

"That's just the beginning. Like our business plan says, we want to start making custom furniture again, under the Barrett's Mill name. Folks love having something unique, and that's what we'll give 'em. Everything will be ripped on the saws and handmade by our own carpenters, so no two pieces will be the same."

"All those shop classes you took are finally coming in handy."

He took her teasing with an easygoing grin. "Yeah, but I've also got a secret weapon."

"What's that?"

Glancing around as if he was checking for spies, he moved close enough that she picked up the scent of soap and hard work. It was a pleasant, masculine kind of smell, totally different from the overbearing colognes so many of her coworkers were convinced women loved. They reeked of trying way too hard, while Paul wasn't trying at all. It set him apart from all the other men she knew, and she sternly dragged her wandering attention back to what he was saying.

"My brother Jason and I have been out in Oregon, working for a company that dredges old timber from river bottoms to be used in modern mills. Back in the day, they used to float trees down from the mountains, and a lot of the bigger ones sank. Some are over a hundred years old, and they're buried in the mud, just waiting for someone to come along and salvage them. I worked out a deal with my old boss, and when we're ready, Jason's gonna bring a load of them here for us to use."

"Is there really a market for that kind of thing?"

"Sure is. That timber's been seasoning a long time, and once you dry it out, it makes great raw material."

"And it has a story to go along with it," she added, allowing herself a little smile. "People love a good story."

"You got that right. But I've been doing this with my own money, and that ran out a couple weeks ago. We need some serious cash to get us back on track."

His explanation tripped a switch in her mind, and things began falling into place. "Is that why you're driving that old sawmill truck?"

"Yeah. When Boyd and I got back here, I sold my crew-cab pickup to a guy over in Cambridge. I really miss that truck," he admitted with a sigh. "But what he paid me got me started here, so it was worth it."

She was struck by his commitment to reviving the mill, and as she considered what he'd already accomplished on a shoestring budget, she realized his innovative idea just might fly. In the current era of mass-produced everything, people craved one-of-a-kind items that set them apart from the crowd. As Paul continued explaining the nuts and bolts to her, his eagerness began to erode her professional skepticism.

If his motivation had been purely profit, she would've remained pessimistic about his chances. But he'd sacrificed his beloved truck, which proved to her that money was no more important to him now than it had been years ago. Since the tireless effort he was putting in was inspired by the grandfather he adored, she knew Paul would do everything in his power to be successful.

When he finally stopped, she said, "You'd build your marketing strategy around the distinctive history of the town, I assume."

He hesitated, and she knew she'd caught him on that

one. True to form, though, he grinned. "I'll leave that to the experts. My job is to give them something interesting to market."

Good answer. Then again, the natural scholar and superjock she remembered from high school had always had a ready comeback for everything. The guy was a born salesman, but where the bank's money was concerned, she wasn't certain that what he was selling was worth buying into.

"It's not up to me." His cocky grin faded a bit, and she felt a prick of guilt for dashing his hopes. She felt an obligation to be honest with him, but reopening the shuttered business clearly meant a lot to him. Out of respect for his feelings, she softened her tone. "I'll do my appraisal, then present it to the loan committee for their consideration. The notes and pictures I'm taking today will help them make a fair decision."

"But you can sway them with the way you lay things out, right?"

The suddenly desperate edge to his voice didn't jibe with the laid-back personality he'd displayed until now. It made her uncomfortable, and out of habit, she fell back on her usual detachment. "Sometimes. For now, I should get back to work."

"Okay. I'll be in here tinkering, so let me know if you need anything."

As she resumed her assessment, she began to rethink her initial gut reaction. On paper, Barrett's Sawmill was the worst kind of project the bank could take on. But having viewed it in person, she definitely saw potential in the old mill and its new owner.

The problem was, if Paul couldn't turn a profit and defaulted on the loan, the loss would be a black mark against her. But if she championed his idea and he succeeded, she'd look like a financial whiz. Then she'd have a realistic shot at the vice president's position opening up when the head of her department retired at the end of the year. This could be precisely what she needed to make a lasting impression on her father and move her one precious step closer to her ultimate goal of running the bank someday.

Cautious by nature, this was a thorny decision for her, but she was starting to believe the possible benefit just might outweigh the risk. The trick would be convincing a room full of ultraconservative bankers to agree with her.

Chelsea Barnes, Paul thought while he painstakingly sharpened an old saw blade one tooth at a time. Of all the people Theo Barnes could've sent to do this appraisal, who'd have guessed he'd choose his tightly wound daughter?

While his visitor poked around, taking electronic notes on her tablet and snapping pictures with a slick digital 35 mm camera, Paul tried not to watch her, but it was tough. Somewhere along the line, the crazy-smart bookworm that lingered in his adolescent memories had become one of the most beautiful women he'd ever met.

Not gorgeous like a model, he amended silently. She was too petite for that. But the gray suit and crisp white blouse she wore set off her expertly twisted auburn hair and vibrant green eyes to perfection. The earrings sparkling in the sunlight were obviously diamonds, and more studded the slender gold watch that had probably cost more than he made in a month. The two of them might've started out in the same tiny town, but they'd ended up at completely opposite ends of the spectrum.

As she prowled around his domain, those keen eyes didn't seem to miss a thing, lighting with curiosity while she examined the machinery, narrowing when she glanced into the darkness beyond the production area.

"What's back there?" she asked, pointing with her stylus.

"I call it the tomb," he joked. "Even Boyd won't go back there."

Clearly unamused, she angled a look at him, one elegant brow lifted in reproach. "That's nearly half your available floor space and will be included in the appraisal. If you don't currently have it in your plans, we'll want to invent a use for it before the board reviews your request."

Paul couldn't believe his ears. Was the ice princess of Barrett's Mill High actually stepping down from her glacier to help a peasant? His attitude must have showed, because she turned to face him head-on.

She didn't look happy. "Did I say something funny?"

"No. Why?"

"You were grinning," she said haughtily, tilting her cute little nose in the air. "I'm totally serious about this. You should be, too."

She'd been serious about everything when they were growing up, too, he recalled grimly. Always studying, never allowing anyone to discover if she had a lighter side. Chilled by her frosty glare, Paul decided that despite the smile she'd given him earlier, she hadn't changed all that much. Not that it mattered to him either way. The only approval he needed from her was financial.

When Boyd ambled over to say hello to her, Paul warned, "Not now, boy. The lady has work to do."

To his amazement, she crouched down and offered a

delicate hand to the lumbering hound. "Oh, I can take a break. Boyd, is it?"

The big oaf woofed at her and collapsed onto his side in a shameless plea for a belly rub. With a quick laugh, she obliged. "There's a good boy. How did you end up here, anyway?"

"You mean, with me?" Paul poked a little fun at himself, hoping to share in her suddenly generous mood. "He wandered into the logging camp I was working at, half-starved but friendly as could be. I shared a cheeseburger with him, and here we are."

She gazed up at him with something he'd never expected to see from her in a million years: respect. "You saved his life. That's amazing."

Actually, Boyd had done more for Paul than the other way around, but he wasn't comfortable telling her that. Instead, he shrugged. "He's a great dog, and he deserved a chance."

"But you're the one who gave it to him," she pressed, standing to look Paul squarely in the eye. He couldn't imagine what might be going through that pretty head of hers right now, but he was fairly certain he was better off not knowing. In his experience, once you assumed you could determine what a woman was thinking, it was a sure sign you were headed for trouble.

Big trouble.

Hoping to appear nonchalant, he folded his arms and leaned against a support post. "So, any ideas for what I should claim I'm gonna do with that back room?"

After a moment, she replied, "It should be something that generates revenue aside from the furniture business. The idea is to broaden your appeal and be less at the mercy of the outside retail market. An area for woodworking classes or a gift shop that sells specialty items people can only get here or on your website, something like that."

"Huh. I've done a lotta things in my life, but I'm not much of a teacher, and I wouldn't even know where to start designing a website."

"If you don't mind me asking," she said, "what *have* you been doing?"

"Let's see. When I was in Oklahoma, I worked in the oil fields. In Missouri, I did some long-haul trucking. In Colorado, I worked on an alpaca farm."

"Seriously?"

"Yeah. Word of advice—they might look cute, but they're nasty when you rile 'em." That got him a flicker of a grin, and he was pretty proud of himself. Until she gave him one of those troublemaker looks that made any guy with half a brain want to squirm.

"Maybe you know someone who could help you with the retail part," she said with an odd glint in her eyes.

Crazy as it seemed, he wondered if she was fishing for details on his personal life. He wasn't sure why she cared, but he decided to play along, just for fun.

Rubbing his chin, he pretended to consider her suggestion. "Maybe I do. Could be dangerous to ask her, though, seeing as the last time I saw her she was in Phoenix, tossing my stuff out a window and chucking a lamp at my head."

That got him a withering feminine glare that made him feel about six inches tall. "I can't begin to imagine why."

Her response caught him off guard, and he bristled defensively, which was completely out of character for him. Most of the time, he couldn't care less what other people thought of him. Why did this snippy woman's opinion matter so much? "That's kinda harsh, don't you think?"

"Men are all the same," she informed him, as if he needed the lesson and it was up to her to enlighten him. "You're big teddy bears until something doesn't go your way, then you're on your way out the door. It's a wonder any of you ever grow up enough to amount to anything."

"Hey, *she* kicked *me* out." He pointed to his chest for emphasis.

Chelsea's eyes sparked like furious emeralds. "Did you ever ask her why?"

"Not that it's any of your business, but she traded me in for a guy with a Porsche. When I called her a greedy gold digger, she didn't take it well." It still stung that what he'd had to offer her hadn't been enough. The blow to his ego hadn't quite healed, and he was determined to avoid a repeat performance.

"So you just walked out, packed up your truck and went to Oregon?" When he didn't respond, she shook her head at him. "Same old Paul. Never happy with where you are, always looking over the horizon for something better."

The fact that she was at least partially right didn't help his suddenly sour mood. "You haven't changed, either. You're still judging other people for taking risks you'd never even dream of. How's that working for you?"

Dismissing him, she pivoted on one of her fancy shoes and went down a set of steps to the side yard where they used to unload the trucks. Paul stood there for a while, trying to get control of his boiling temper before he made the situation worse by charging after her to continue their…argument? No, that wasn't quite it, he admitted as he watched her through a window. It had been more like sparring, each of them testing the other before squaring up to land their best punches.

Just like old times, he thought with a grimace. Her last name happened to come before his in the alphabet, so they'd often been teamed up for school projects. Their efforts had ended up being more competitions than collaborations, and although they'd scored well, every second they were forced to work together had been a teeth-grinding clash of wills. Now he needed her help or this restoration was dead in the water. Paul simply couldn't let that happen.

After battling cancer for five years, Granddad's fight was rapidly coming to an end, and all he wanted was to see his cherished mill up and running before he died. Paul had driven across the country to make sure that happened, which meant he had to man up and apologize to Chelsea for insulting her. Searching for inspiration, he glanced down at Boyd, who was stretched out in a patch of late-morning sunlight, his brow wrinkled with what could only be described as concern. More than once, it had flashed through Paul's mind that his canine buddy was more sympathetic than a lot of people he knew.

"Whattya say, partner? Wanna go make nice for me?" Boyd let out a quiet groan, then closed his eyes to resume his nap. "Yeah, well, thanks for nothin'."

Groveling really shouldn't be all that tough for him, he reasoned as he followed after Chelsea. He'd begged forgiveness from so many women over the years, he'd gotten pretty good at it. But as he watched her with her rolling measuring stick and camera, so intent on her task that she didn't appear to notice him, his gut warned him that this time would be different.

Because she was brighter than most, and she'd see right through his usual I'm-just-a-guy approach. That meant he'd have to go with the truth, which could be dicey when it came to the female species. But this wasn't about him, he reminded himself as he glanced back at the half-restored mill. It was about answering Granddad's prayers to get the family business back in working order. If Paul had to eat a little humble pie in the meantime, it was best to choke it down as quickly as possible and watch his mouth from here on out.

Hoping to appear contrite, he shoved his hands in the pockets of his jeans and trudged down the steps. In the yard, he intercepted Chelsea. Summoning every sad moment of his life into his expression, he kept it simple. "I'm sorry."

"For what?" she countered tartly. "Being you? Please."

Sharp words leaped onto his tongue, and he sent up a quick prayer for patience. What he said to her right now would make or break this project, and he wasn't averse to calling in a little divine help. "For being out of line. You obviously have a great life, and I had no right to talk to you that way. I hope you can forgive me."

The change in her was remarkable. He'd braced himself for a scolding, but what he got instead was a slowly dawning smile. By the time it reached her eyes, he glimpsed a sparkle in them he'd never seen before. How many guys had gotten that view of her? he wondered briefly before slamming the door on his curiosity. He had no intention of going anywhere remotely personal with her, so there was no point in even asking the question.

"Thank you, Paul. That can't have been easy for you to do, and I appreciate it. Believe it or not," she added in a warmer tone, "I think your idea for this place has a lot of merit."

"That's good," Paul stammered, unable to believe what he was hearing.

She gave him a nod, then got back to her measuring. While he appreciated her attempt to be encouraging, he was smart enough to realize it didn't mean much in this situation. When it came to dollars and cents, banks were notoriously hard-hearted these days, which didn't bode well for the Barretts.

It wasn't himself he was worried about, Paul thought morosely. He'd failed before—plenty of times—and as Chelsea had so deftly noted, he had a knack for burying his mistakes and moving on.

But this time, he had to succeed. Knowing that scared him to death.

Chapter Two

When Chelsea was finished with her survey, she stopped in the millhouse to say goodbye to Paul. "Thanks for the tour. The loan committee will be meeting tomorrow, and I'll make my presentation then. You should have an answer by midweek."

Paul looked up from the doohickey he was oiling with a grim expression. "I can tell by your tone you don't think we should get our hopes up."

She did, but she was usually better at hiding her opinion from clients. Either he was unusually adept at reading her, or she was losing her touch. Whichever it was, she wasn't thrilled to learn she'd let her emotions show. Hoping to ease the blow, she sat down on an overturned crate beside him. "I won't lie to you, Paul. With the economy the way it is, projects like these are rejected more often than not."

"But this one's special," he insisted, his dark eyes pleading with her for something she couldn't give him. "There was nothing around here until my family built this mill. That has to count for something."

Unfortunately, there were hundreds of villages just

like it scattered throughout the country, fading from memory because they weren't deemed important enough to save. But she couldn't bear to tell him that, so she hedged. "I'll do my best, but I can't make any promises. You need to understand that."

"Sure," he breathed, his shoulders lifting and then drooping with a heavy sigh.

The defeated pose was far removed from the arrogant sports star she remembered from high school, and she felt her heart going out to him. Firmly, she put a stop to that and reminded herself this was a business proposition. Where money was concerned, she had to keep a cool head at all times. She was on pace to be the youngest vice president in the long history of Shenandoah Bank and Trust, and she had no intention of losing sight of her goal when she had it within her grasp. Because, quite honestly, she had few friends outside of work and an almost nonexistent social life. Without her career, she was nothing.

"I'll get back to Roanoke and start processing your files," she said as she stood. "Have a good day."

"You, too," he muttered without looking up. Chelsea decided that was the best she could expect considering she'd just crushed his dreams, so she headed for the door. She was on the porch when he called out her name.

She backtracked, and he gave her a sheepish grin as he got to his feet. "That's no way to treat a lady, and I apologize. Let me walk you to your car."

"You don't—"

"Yeah, I do. If Mom found out I booted you outta here, she'd tan my hide."

Chelsea wouldn't be talking to anyone else before leaving town, so there was little chance of his mother learning about their awkward reunion. Then again, she mused while they strode outside, this was Barrett's Mill. Someone had probably noticed her on the road and begun spreading the word that she'd come back, however briefly. The idea tickled her for some reason, and while she normally detested anyone poking their nose into her affairs, she had to laugh.

"What?" Paul asked, glancing around to see what had amused her.

"Just thinking about how this place never changes."

"Yeah, that's what I like most about it."

Bewildered by his attitude, she didn't bother to hide her reaction. "Really? Doesn't it drive you crazy?"

"Sure, but that's part of its charm." Leaning against a gnarled old oak, he folded his arms and gave her the same wide-open country-boy grin he'd worn all through high school. "I've lived lots of places, but I always come back here because it's home."

"This is my first visit since we graduated," she blurted without thinking.

"Doesn't surprise me any," he said with a frown. "Even when we were kids, you wanted more than you could find here."

"There's a big, fascinating world out there."

Studying her for a long moment, he murmured, "But you haven't found what you're looking for yet. Why is that?"

His perceptiveness unnerved her almost as much as his appallingly blunt—and highly personal—question. She'd usually ignore such an intrusion, but she didn't want him thinking for even one second that he'd rattled her. "I don't see how that's any of your business."

"Just curious. Have a good trip back."

This time she didn't linger out of politeness but opened

the driver's door and gratefully sank into the buttery leather seat. Eager to leave the mill and its aggravating caretaker behind, she angrily punched the button to start the engine.

Nothing.

Gritting her teeth in frustration, she reset the electronic fob and tried the button again, with the same result. The dealer had done a full service on this car just last week, and now it wouldn't start when she was in the absolute middle of nowhere? Could this day possibly get any worse?

The answer to that question loomed in her window, and for a few immature seconds, she ignored Paul's irritating presence. Then she realized she was being ridiculous and hit the control to lower the window. It wouldn't work, of course, and she reluctantly climbed out of her worthless car to face the music.

"Problem?" he asked, a teasing glint in his eyes.

"It won't start, as you can see. You're good with mechanical things," she said hopefully. "Could you please take a look?"

"Well, since you said 'please,' I'll give it a shot. Pop the hood."

She did as he asked, standing helplessly while he pushed it open and peered inside. The baffled look on his face spoke volumes, and he gave a long, dubious whistle. "You need a computer to talk to a car like this. Fred Morgan might be able to get it running, though."

"Great. Let's call him."

Squinting up at the sky, Paul shook his head. "We could, but it's lunchtime, and he'll be at The Whistlestop. We'll find him there."

Chelsea didn't like what he was implying. They'd had

a few nice moments, but otherwise the man grated on her every nerve. She hadn't planned on spending any more time with him than strictly necessary. "We?"

"I'm headed there anyway, so I can give you a ride. Unless you'd rather walk." Angling his head, he gave her high heels an uncertain look.

"Can't you just send Fred out here? I mean, after you've both eaten," she added so she didn't sound quite so desperate.

"Are you serious?" Paul's eyes roamed around the deserted property before settling on her. "There's no way I'm leaving you out here alone. Boyd's a great watchdog, but he's not much in the protection department. He loves everyone he meets."

Chelsea didn't think anything would happen to her, but she yielded to the wisdom of what he was saying. These days, a girl couldn't be too careful. So, since she was out of options, she decided to make the best of a bad situation. "All right, then. I appreciate the offer."

"And lunch," he said, motioning her toward his truck. "By the looks of that suit, you don't eat near as much as you should."

Appalled by his comment, she pulled up short. "Are you saying I'm too thin?"

"Got that right." The dented passenger door groaned loudly as he opened it for her. "Some of Molly Harkness's chicken and dumplings should do the trick."

Oh, the Southern diet, Chelsea lamented. She loved the taste of fried anything smothered in gravy, but the effect it had on her waistline was another issue altogether. "I'll just get a salad, thanks," she announced as she sat on the threadbare seat.

"Over my dead body," he grumbled, shutting the door

and climbing in the other side. Raising an eyebrow at her, he crossed his fingers and turned the key. After a few tries, the cranky engine roared to life, and Paul circled the turnaround and headed for the main road.

"You're not really going to try and tell me what to eat, are you?" she demanded.

"Somebody should." Eyeing her in the rearview mirror, he shook his head. "When's the last time you had a steak?"

She honestly couldn't recall, but she wasn't about to admit that to him. Instead, she disregarded the question and used the old-fashioned handle to roll her window down. A breeze scented with wild roses and honeysuckle drifted into the cab, and she took a deep breath of it. "It smells like summer, doesn't it?"

"Sure does." Pointing over to the right, he said, "I cleared a path along the creek last week. Boyd loves it, and it gives me a break from all that oil and sawdust."

"That sounds nice." Secretly, she envied him his flexible schedule. While he was working very hard, it was on his own terms, not dictated by someone else's clock.

"My brothers and I used to have a lot of fun at that old swimming hole down at the other end," Paul continued. "We'd grab some watermelons and a radio, then meet our friends there in the morning and not go home till dark. Those were some good times."

His nostalgic rambling trailed off, and he tuned the radio to a local station. It was noon, and while the national anthem played, Chelsea realized she'd missed a lot by being so driven during high school. Friends, fun and lazy days at the swimming hole. If she'd known then what she knew now, she'd have enjoyed herself more.

"Chelsea," Paul said gently, as if her silence made him

uncomfortable. When she met his eyes, he went on. "Not everything here was bad, y'know."

"I didn't say it was bad," she corrected him. "I said it was limited."

"Uh-huh. And how's the world treating you these days?"

"Fine." That got her a skeptical look, and she couldn't help laughing at herself. "Okay, it's tough. But I'll figure it out."

Eventually.

"When you do, clue me in, would ya?"

"Like you'd ever need help from me," she scoffed. "Mr. Valedictorian and MVP of everything."

"That was a long time ago," he reminded her in a somber tone. "A lot's changed since then."

The unexpected confession piqued her curiosity, and despite her vow to remain detached, she couldn't help wondering what he was referring to. "Such as?"

After a moment, he slanted her another one of those maddening grins. "Such as, when did you get so gorgeous? Last I knew, you were this shy thing with thick glasses and a book in front of her face all the time."

She wasn't falling for that lethal Barrett charm. He and his brothers had been dipped in it at birth, and she didn't doubt that most women went for it in a big way. Not her, though. She recognized trouble when she saw it and had always preferred to give those boys a wide berth. But she wasn't too mature to admit that knowing he thought she'd grown out of her ugly-duckling phase pleased her immensely. "I got contacts and learned to be more assertive. Don't forget, I skipped a grade, so I was a year younger than all of you."

"Smart as a whip, that's what I remember," he commented with what sounded like genuine admiration. "You scared the rest of us to death."

"And you blew the curve for our class GPA. I had to work like a dog to keep up with you, and you never cracked a book. It was completely unfair."

"Keep up with me?" he echoed as he left the wooded road and pulled onto the upper end of Main Street. "Were we competing or something?"

"Of course we were." Exasperated by his lack of understanding, she blew out a frustrated breath. "You were one of five kids, and if you messed up, one of your brothers could pick up the slack. I was an only child, so I had to get everything just right. The top colleges love valedictorians, and that meant I had to be one. Period, end of story."

"Well, now, that explains a lot."

As he parked the truck along the curb, she nailed him with her coolest look. "What's that supposed to mean?"

Unfazed, he swiveled to face her and opened his mouth to speak. Then he apparently changed his mind and shook his head. "Forget I mentioned it. Let's eat."

Ordinarily, she wouldn't let him off the hook so easily. But the chances of them seeing one another after today were infinitesimal, so she decided to let the argument drop. Once her car was fixed, she promised herself, she'd head back to Roanoke, where she belonged. And stay there.

Hailing from the days when the railroad churned its way through Barrett's Mill, The Whistlestop was a historic gem. Some enterprising old-timer had purchased a heap of a trolley car, gutted the interior and placed it on a section of track parallel to the sidewalk to form the front of the most unique restaurant she'd ever eaten at.

Behind it was a modest-sized building people flocked to from all over, just to sample some of the owners' mouth-watering down-home cooking.

Like the rest of the town, it hadn't changed much, but the oval sign over the entryway caught her eye. With beveled edges and an antiqued finish, it showed an artist's rendering of the building over a stylized script that was old-fashioned but easily readable from a distance. The combination of traditional and modern was the ideal effect for the diner that anchored the town's tiny business district.

"Who did the new sign?" she asked.

"No idea. Ask Molly."

Despite their terse exchange, he politely circled the truck and helped her out. As Chelsea stepped down, she caught a whiff of fresh corn bread and barbecue that made her stomach rumble with anticipation.

Obviously, he noticed it, because he pulled open the vintage glass-front door with a chuckle. "What was that you were saying about a salad?"

Just this once, she thought. After all, a little Southern food wouldn't ruin her diet forever. Although she detested being wrong, she gave in and laughed at the smug expression he was wearing. "Maybe I'll take a peek at the menu, just to be on the safe side."

"Good choice. Hey, Molly!" Peering over a set of swinging doors into the kitchen, he held up a hand in greeting. "Come see who I found wandering the old mill road."

Molly Harkness was all of five feet tall, and she had to prop one of the doors open to discover what was up. When she caught sight of Chelsea, her face brightened with delight. Pushing between two busboys, she emerged wearing a flour-covered apron that proclaimed her Best Grandmama Ever. "Is that Chelsea Lynn Barnes I'm lookin' at?"

Paul's use of her full name earlier had irked her. Hearing it now, spoken with such affection, made her smile. "Yes, ma'am. How've you been?"

"Oh, peachy, like always." After giving her a warm hug, Molly assessed her with disdain. "What? They don't feed you up there in Roanoke?"

"Not like this." Chelsea paused for a long sniff. "What've you got going back there?"

She beamed proudly. "Bruce's doin' up some fresh barbecue pork and chicken with a new recipe he invented last night. Y'all pick a table, and I'll get you some sweet tea while you check over the menu."

"You don't have to—" Before Chelsea could finish, their hostess was gone in a puff of flour.

"I get it," Paul muttered as they headed into the dining room. "I comment on your weight, you smack me down. Molly does it, you agree with her."

"It's all in the delivery."

The place was packed, but there was a table for two at the far end. While Paul ushered her through the crowd, several people stopped them to say hello. Most of them were familiar old faces locked in her memory all these years. Some had changed slightly, but others were exactly as she remembered them. One of those was Pastor Griggs, who was having lunch at a corner table. When he stood to greet her, she felt a little awkward. Growing up she'd attended Sunday school and services at the Crossroads Church faithfully every week. Now, not so much. She wondered if he could tell.

"It's wonderful to see you again," he told her, grasping both of her hands with a fatherly smile. "How does it feel to be home?"

It had been ages since she thought of Barrett's Mill the way Paul did, but now that the pastor mentioned it, she didn't consider anywhere else home, either. She hadn't realized it until this moment, and it rattled her enough that she had to kick her brain back into conversation mode. "Good. I'm not staying long, just helping Paul out with something at the mill."

"Yes, the loan," the preacher said, nodding somberly. "Every other bank in the area turned them down, and we're all praying your father can help. Will's done so much for the town, and we want to see him happy. Not to mention getting some tourists to stop here would really help us out moneywise."

The revelation was news to Chelsea, and she wasn't sure how to respond. She'd had no idea the entire village was in on this. The fact that so many people stood behind the mill put a whole different spin on it for her, giving her a glimpse into the pressure Paul must feel to make the project successful. Beyond that, his application had become more to her than debits and credits on a ledger sheet. "Ultimately, the board makes the decision, so I can't promise anything. But I'll do my best."

"God bless you both." After placing a hand on her shoulder and the other on Paul's, he returned to his meal.

"Well, that was awkward," Chelsea murmured as she and Paul seated themselves on opposite sides of the tiny booth.

Already nose-deep in the menu, he asked, "Why?"

Sensing that he hadn't strayed as far from their Christian upbringing as she had, she wisely kept her mouth shut. But he was still the same old Paul, and he eyed her suspiciously. Setting down his menu, he folded his well-muscled forearms on top and leaned in with a slight grin. "You're not tight with the big guy anymore?"

"I wouldn't have phrased it quite that way," she chided, relenting when his grin widened into a you-can't-fool-me look. "All right, you nailed me on that one. Happy?"

"Immensely. Most women baffle me, but you haven't changed a bit. It's kinda nice."

"I've changed plenty," she insisted as Molly showed up with a pitcher of tea and two glasses. "You're exactly the same, though."

"You make that sound like a bad thing."

"Trust me, it is."

"Arguing again?" Molly teased, pulling an order pad from the pocket of her apron. "It feels like old times, seeing you kids in my place. What'll you have?"

"How 'bout some barbecue?" Paul suggested with a questioning look at Chelsea. "If you want, we can get one chicken and one pork and split 'em."

What did she care? With all the trouble he was causing her, she'd have boatloads of pent-up aggravation for working off the calories at the gym later. "Sure, with coleslaw. And double fries with gravy," she added impulsively.

Beaming proudly, Molly patted her back. "Good for you, hon. You only go around once, so you might as well eat what you want. These'll be out shortly."

"Before you go, I was wondering who did your new sign. It's really unique."

"Jenna Reed blew into town a few months back," Molly explained. "She's one of those traveling-artist types, y'know, the kind who sell their stuff at a roadside stand. Anyway, she came in here one day and asked if I knew anyone who was looking for some new signage."

"And you hired her," Paul guessed. "Out of the goodness of your heart."

"The girl needed to pay her rent, and our old plaque was falling off the hooks. She didn't charge much, and we get all kinds of compliments about it. I'd say we got the better end of the bargain."

"That sign at the mill is way past its prime," Chelsea told Paul. "You might want to contact Jenna and see if she can help you out. You really need a logo to brand your products and marketing materials."

"Great idea." Grabbing a napkin, he borrowed Molly's pen and wrote down the woman's info. Once she'd gone, he refolded his arms and leaned closer. "You've always been a by-the-numbers type. Where'd you pick up your eye for artistic stuff?"

That he'd noticed the change, and obviously approved of it, gave her shaky ego a pleasant little boost. The fact that those deep brown eyes were twinkling at her had nothing to do with it, of course, but it was nice to be recognized for something she'd done rather than how pretty she looked. She got her fill of that at the bank, and it was refreshing to be praised for stepping out of her usual realm of expertise.

"Marketing's always interested me," she confided for the very first time. Even her father didn't know, because to him, banking was the only industry worth pursuing. "I like analyzing the unique aspects of a company and figuring out how to play them up to their best advantage."

"Like earlier, when you asked about my plans for promoting the mill," he said as he filled their glasses with tea. "Do you do that often?"

"Never." Hearing the edge to her tone, she did her

best to dial it back. "Our clients aren't interested in my opinion on that kind of thing. They hire experts for that."

"Your mom was a real creative lady. You must've gotten your talent from her."

The mention of her long-absent mother hit Chelsea like a bucket of ice water, and she felt herself stiffen in self-defense. She recognized that it was absurd to tense up that way, but it was reflexive and she simply couldn't help it. Hoping to disguise her reaction, she shrugged as if it didn't matter much to her. "Probably."

"Where is she these days?"

"Australia, with husband number four." Or was it Austria? It had been months since her last email, and she honestly couldn't recall where Mom had said they were living now.

"Cool place. You should go visit her when you get a chance."

"I haven't been invited," Chelsea spat with more venom than she'd intended. Swallowing some tea, she went on. "Beyond that, I haven't seen her since I was fourteen. After the divorce, she and Dad could hardly look at each other without snarling."

In truth, they'd been like that her entire life, and the breakup of their marriage had been a relief for all of them. Paul seemed to sense that, because the look on his face shifted from polite interest to genuine sympathy. Considering the fact that they'd been wrangling all morning, his compassion touched her deeply. In her fast-paced world, people flew past each other with a quick greeting, seldom pausing for a meaningful conversation. Something told her if she wanted to keep talking, he'd go right on listening, nodding and encouraging until she was finished. Part of her longed to do just that, but logic took over, reminding her the last thing she needed was to allow herself to become personally involved with a potential client. Especially this one.

He'd be easier to dismiss if he were still the same arrogant jock she knew years ago. The kind, caring man who'd taken his place was a temptation any woman with a pulse would have a hard time resisting.

Chelsea twisted in her seat to survey the crowd. "I don't see Fred anywhere."

"Must be out somewhere helping somebody else. I'll give him a call after we order." As if on cue, his cell phone rang, and he checked the caller ID. "It's Gram. I can take it outside if you want."

The sudden worry that creased his forehead reinforced her hunch that there was more to the mill project than he'd claimed, and she waved away his offer. "No, go ahead."

"Hey, there. What's up with my favorite girl today?" Listening for a few moments, his frown hardened with determination. "Is that right? Well, put the nurse on." Another pause. "I realize you're the professional here, but Will's an eighty-five-year-old man who doesn't know how much longer he's got. If he wants barbecue ribs, he should have 'em. Yes, I take full responsibility for disobeying doctor's orders. You're welcome."

Will Barrett was dying.

Reality struck her with the force of a physical blow, and Chelsea felt her heart seize in her chest. Too shocked for words, she gasped something even she couldn't understand. Part shock, part sob, it was all she could manage, and Paul held up a hand to keep her from speaking.

"Gram, we're good to go, and I'll bring a meal for you,

too." Checking the desserts board, he asked, "Rhubarb pie or triple berry? Got it. See ya soon."

Closing his phone, he clasped it in his hands, staring down at the maze place mat on the table in front of him. All the bravado seemed to have drained out of him, and he closed his eyes with a weary sigh. The anguish on his face tugged at Chelsea's closely guarded heart, and she searched for some comforting words. None came to mind, but she couldn't just sit there and watch him suffer this way.

Even though she'd resolved to remain objective about this unusual assignment, it had suddenly become very personal. Reaching over, she rested her hand over both of his, wishing there was something more she could do.

Chapter Three

When he looked up, Paul noticed tears shining in Chelsea's eyes. Considering the fact that they'd been sparring with each other most of the morning, it seemed odd that she'd feel sorry for him. But the way he was feeling right now, he'd take any sympathy she cared to offer him.

"The doctors can't do anything more for Granddad's cancer," he explained, "and he's accepted that he's not gonna beat it this time. The last thing he wants before he goes is to see the mill up and running again. Well, that and some Whistlestop barbecue," he added with a wry grin.

"Is that why you're staying with them instead of at your parents' place over in Cambridge?"

"Yeah. Mom and my sisters-in-law take turns dropping by during the days, but we all feel better knowing someone's around if Gram needs a hand at night."

Swallowing some tea, she said, "I'd like to stop in and see them, if you don't mind giving me a ride over there."

Seeing as she was in such a hurry to get back, he was stunned that she was willing to delay her trip. Stunned and more than a little impressed. Maybe the ice princess had a heart after all, he thought with a grin. "Don't mind a bit. They've been feeling a little cooped up lately, and I'm sure they'd love to see you. Then we'll track down Fred and get your car back on the road."

"Thanks." Swirling her straw around, she asked, "Is it true all the banks around here turned you down?"

"Yup," he replied, popping a saltine into his mouth. "They said it's 'cause the only collateral I have is the mill, and it's not enough to make up for me not knowing the first thing about running a business."

"And if Shenandoah Bank turns you down? What then?"

"I don't wanna think about it." When a waitress arrived with their order, he added the take-out meals to their tab and turned the conversation to a more positive subject. "So, tell me what's been going on with you. Senior year you were voted most likely to be the first woman president. Have you picked your running mate yet?"

She laughed, which had been his intent. It was a shame to see those incredible eyes filled with anything but joy. "Why? Are you interested in the job?"

"Not a chance." Forking up some of the chicken from her platter, he plopped it onto his and did the opposite with his pork. "I'd be a terror in those meetings, knocking heads together all day long."

"Interesting strategy. They might actually accomplish something that way." Munching a gravy-smothered fry, she hummed in appreciation. "I forgot how much I love this kind of food."

"We can get some for you to take back, if you want."

"No, thanks. I'll be making up for this on the treadmill for the next week as it is."

"Your call."

They chatted their way through lunch, and Paul couldn't help admiring the classy woman seated opposite him. He'd never been interested in her before, but for some reason, now he was captivated. The problem was, she was too smart for her own good, and out of respect for his sanity, he made it a policy to avoid women like her. They were way too much work.

But that didn't mean he couldn't be friendly. Not that he'd try to charm her into helping him out with the bank or anything, but it couldn't hurt to be nice. The old flies-and-honey saying popped into his mind, and he grinned. He was pretty sure Chelsea would object to being compared to insects of any kind.

"What?" she demanded with a frown. "Have I got sauce on my chin or something?"

"No, I was just thinking about how funny it is we reconnected after all these years."

"Funny ha-ha or funny ironic?"

"Both." Holding up his glass, he said, "To old enemies getting a fresh start."

"We weren't enemies, really," she corrected him with a little grin. "More like rivals who were going after the same things from different directions."

"To old rivals, then. I pity anyone dumb enough to try to keep you from getting what you want."

"That I can drink to," she agreed, clinking glasses to seal the toast.

Paul heard another click and glanced over to find Molly standing in the middle of the dining room with a digital camera in her hand. "That's a good one."

"For what?" Chelsea asked, apparently as confused as Paul was.

"For my collection." Pointing to a collage made up of

old, fading photos, she explained, "I've been adding in new pictures of the people up there, like a history album of the town."

Playing along, Paul faked a horrified gasp. "We're not really in that, are we?"

"Of course you are."

Plucking one from the wall, she handed the picture to him, and he angled it so Chelsea could see, too. Sure enough, there they were, perched on stools at the lunch counter, deep in a debate about something or other. You could tell because Paul was waving his hands and grinning while Chelsea glared at him with the kind of look that could freeze Sterling Creek in the dead of summer. Between them were two melting sundaes, forgotten in their quest to win the latest in a series of arguments that had lasted from junior high straight through to graduation.

"It's one of my favorites." Molly took the photo back and gave them each a warm smile. "Sometimes I wonder how things would've worked out if you two could quit beating on each other long enough to realize how much alike you are."

They both laughed, and Paul echoed, "Alike? Ya gotta be kidding."

"I'm deadly serious. You're smart as anything and stubborn as a pair of mules. Imagine what you could accomplish if you put aside your pride and pull in the same direction for a change."

With that, she turned and left them staring at each other. If he was reading her expression accurately, Paul was fairly confident that Chelsea was as horrified by that idea as he was. Then Molly's words registered more clearly. "Did you notice how she said that?"

Eyes wide with shock, Chelsea nodded. “She didn’t say ‘accomplished,’ as if she was referring to what happened in the past. She made it sound like we should work together now and see how it goes.”

“Don’t worry about it,” he reassured her smoothly. “Everyone’s got an opinion about this mill project. Doesn’t mean she’s right.”

“Absolutely. Of course.”

While they both continued eating, Paul was careful not to let Chelsea catch him glancing over at her. Because, despite what he’d said just a few moments ago, he couldn’t dismiss the possibility that Molly was right. With his technical know-how and her business sense, he and Chelsea would make a great team. Having her on his side would definitely improve the chances of his wild idea succeeding.

Unfortunately, his male instincts warned him that any partnership with this by-the-books accountant would drive him completely over the edge. Then again, working with a woman instead of dating her would be a refreshing change for him. At least he wouldn’t end up getting tossed out of his own apartment into the rain.

“What a wonderful surprise!” Olivia Barrett exclaimed, folding Chelsea into a warm hug. It was the second one she’d gotten today, and this one felt just as good as the first. To be welcomed back after so many years away felt amazing.

“I was in town, so I wanted to stop by and see you two,” she explained with a hesitant peek into the dining room. All the antique furniture was pushed to one side, opening up space for a hospital bed. “Is this a good time?”

"It's always a good time for company." The shadows beneath her brown eyes spoke of many sleepless nights, but the determined glimmer said she was making the best of their difficult situation. "Folks come tiptoeing in here like Will's already laid out for his funeral. It makes me crazy."

"Well, we're here to fix that," her grandson informed her, holding up two take-out bags printed with The Whistlestop's trolley logo.

"We could smell it when you were coming up the walk. I'll get some plates."

"In here," he replied, wiggling the bags. "No dishes for you to wash, so you can just relax and enjoy your lunch."

"My boy," she cooed, grasping his chin for a fond shake. "Did I ever tell you you're my favorite?"

When she turned to lead them into the dining room, Paul whispered to Chelsea, "She says that to all of us."

Thanks to him, Chelsea was laughing when she saw Will Barrett. His pale face broke into a bright smile, and though he looked achingly frail, he greeted her in the strong baritone voice that used to ring out from the church choir every Sunday. "Marvelous to see you, Chelsea. Come in. Come in."

His hand trembled as he motioned her to the armchair beside his bed, and she sank into it as unexpected emotions clogged her throat. Paul had warned her his grandfather was dying, but she hadn't been prepared for the reality of what that meant. Though it was tucked behind a leafy ficus, she noticed an IV pole holding a bag of dripping medication. Looking from it to Will, the sympathy in his eyes caught her even more off guard.

"I know," he said simply, patting her hand with his. "It's not easy, but we're making the best of things."

"Why are you here instead of in a hospital?" she blurted without thinking first. When she realized what she'd done, she felt herself reddening in embarrassment.

Will chased off her discomfort with a faint laugh. "All that poking and prodding was making me downright ornery. And the food." Condemning it with a sour face, he continued, "I'm happier here, and now Olivia can be comfortable at home instead of driving back and forth to a place full of sick people."

"Gram came down with pneumonia a few weeks ago," Paul explained, pulling some dining chairs over so they could all sit near Will. Winking at her, he added, "Personally, I think she was just looking for an excuse to stay in bed and do crossword puzzles all day."

"Oh, you," she protested, playfully smacking the back of his head.

A few weeks, Chelsea mused while Olivia dished up barbecue for Will and then herself. The time frame rang a bell, and she turned to Paul with newfound respect. "Is that why you came back from Oregon?"

"Mostly I missed Gram's peach cobbler. It's still the best I ever had."

"I could never keep this one full," she said with an adoring look at him. "The whole time he was growing up, the more I cooked, the more he ate."

"Hey, I'm the middle kid. I had to keep getting bigger so they wouldn't all pound me."

"Are your brothers still around?" Chelsea asked.

His eyes darkened to near black, but he quickly masked his reaction with a grin. "Most of 'em. Connor and Greg live over in Cambridge with their families, and Jason's busy loading up my secret weapon for the mill."

"What about Scott?"

Dead silence. It felt as if something had sucked all the air out of the room, and Chelsea wished she could disappear from sight under the old floorboards.

"Scott's still finding his way," Olivia answered quietly. "Lemonade, dear?"

"Yes, thank you."

Deciding not to risk any more blunders, Chelsea sipped her cool drink and listened to the Barretts discuss the goings-on around the town she'd left behind so long ago. While they talked, she gained a fresh appreciation for the commitment Paul had made, seemingly without a second thought.

His vision for the mill seemed long-term, which meant he wasn't planning on going anywhere. He probably had a life out West, but he was forsaking that to be where he was needed most. Sitting here in this sunny room, being entertained by the local gossip, she was struck by a random thought that rattled her right down to her toes.

This was love.

This was what it meant to put someone else before yourself, to value their happiness and well-being as much as you did your own. While Chelsea had always admired and respected her father, as a teenager she'd accepted that his one-track mind was focused on making his bank as profitable as possible. These days they worked in the same building, but they seldom shared moments like this one. To her knowledge, Theo Barnes had never eaten takeout from paper plates and debated whether the new highway project was a good use of county funds or a complete waste of money.

While she was considering that, Paul's phone rang, and he checked the screen. "Fred," he told her, hitting the answer button. "Hey, there. Thanks for getting back to me. Chelsea Barnes is in town, and her fancy new car won't start. It's at the mill, and I'm hoping you can help us out so she can get back to Roanoke sometime today." He glanced up at the antique schoolhouse clock on the wall. "Half hour's fine. See ya then."

Chelsea was perplexed by their short exchange. Granted, she wasn't Miss Fix-It, but from what she'd heard, Paul hadn't offered the mechanic the slightest bit of useful information. "You didn't tell him a thing. How does he know what to bring?"

"I said 'fancy' and 'new,'" Paul pointed out matter-of-factly. "He'll know."

"But—"

"Do you always hassle people who're trying to help you?"

Folding his arms, he leaned back in his chair and cocked his head in a pose that made her think of Boyd when she'd met him that morning. The idea of Paul beginning to resemble his canine friend was more amusing than it should have been, and she couldn't help smiling.

"That's so much better," he praised her with a wide grin. "You really oughta smile more often. It looks good on you."

Maybe when her career started improving, she'd be able to follow his cavalier—and slightly chauvinistic—advice. But she was where she was, and until she clawed her way up to where she wanted to be, she'd be sticking to the serious route. Since she had no intention of sharing the reasons for her attitude with him or anyone else, she forced a polite smile. "Thank you."

"Ouch," he replied with a chuckle. "That's a mind-your-own-business brush-off if ever I heard one. Anything you wanna tell me?"

Not in this lifetime, she wanted to shoot back. Of course, a Southern lady never spoke to anyone that way, so she settled for "No."

He gave her a long, dubious look before standing. "Then we should head out to meet Fred. He'll get you back on the road in no time."

"So nice to see you, dear." Olivia stood and embraced Chelsea again. "Be sure to come by for a visit next time you're in town."

"And bring more barbecue," Will added eagerly.

That wasn't likely to happen, but Chelsea forced a smile and managed to say her goodbyes without a hitch in her voice. As she and Paul walked through the kitchen, she hated to think of how disappointed his grandparents would be when the bank got a good look at the figures on Paul's loan application and turned him down flat.

Outside, she took in the view of a neighborhood that hadn't changed much since her childhood. Sturdy homes, old but well cared for, lined the street like sentinels from another time. Standing by the truck, she inhaled the scent of gardens overflowing with gardenias and roses, with the exotic aroma of jasmine mixed in for effect. "Mmm… that smells good."

Paul sniffed quickly and shrugged. "I guess so. I'm here all the time, so I guess I don't notice it anymore."

"I don't remember this part of town being so pretty. It's really nice."

Closing her door, he balanced his hands on the window frame and gave her a long, slow smile. "Yeah, it is."

For a few moments, they gazed at each other through the open window, almost as if they'd never met before. In a way, she realized, that was true. The brash football captain and the shy bookworm they'd once been existed in the past, and the people who'd replaced them were all but strangers.

Could they become more than that? a tiny voice in her head wondered.

She pushed the thought firmly back into the depths of her brain, where it belonged. Getting to the top of her profession was her only goal right now, and she couldn't afford any distractions, no matter how handsome they might be.

Paul's pensive look gave way to the nonchalant one he'd been wearing most of the day. On their way out into the country, they drove beneath enormous trees that had withstood the devastating war that had left so much of Virginia stripped and in ruins. Both sides had done their share of damage, and men had returned to a barren wasteland begging for redemption.

With the need for lumber so high, Gideon Barrett and his two surviving brothers sank their meager fortunes into constructing a mill to turn the area's plentiful trees into raw material for new houses, stores, even railroad ties.

In its way, the mill had saved the ravaged town from fading into oblivion. It seemed fitting, somehow, that the residents were fighting to save the landmark business that had given rise to the village they called home. Beyond that, she knew helping the Barretts was the right thing to do.

Tossing aside her pledge to remain cautiously neutral, she said, "Okay, I'm on board. It won't be easy, but I'll figure out a way to get you the money you need for your furniture business. You have my word on it."

Sliding her an incredulous look, he asked, "Did I miss

something? What happened to the numbers not adding up and all?"

"They still don't, and I have a hunch they never will. It would be a unique operation, and there's nothing in the area to compare it to."

"Which means we can't prove it's a profitable idea."

He'd all but admitted this wasn't his area of expertise, but she had to give him credit—he caught on fast. "Exactly."

"You're the logical type," he pressed, obviously still confused. "Formulas and algorithms, they're your thing. What changed your mind?"

Sighing, she met his eyes in the rearview mirror. "I'm doing it for Will."

"So'm I." Paul's grim expression brightened into the crooked grin she remembered from high school. "Looks like we've finally got something in common. If Molly finds out, she'll never let us hear the end of it."

After resisting his many charms all morning, Chelsea eased up on her well-honed discipline and gave him a genuine smile. "I won't tell her if you don't."

"Deal."

Chapter Four

Chelsea spent several hours framing Paul's proposal in as positive a light as she could manage without actually inventing facts. To avoid creating the impression that she was somehow personally invested in the project, she called it Barrett's Mill Restoration and played up the potential she'd observed during her tour. Five minutes before her presentation, she was still tinkering with the conclusion, choosing her words carefully to ensure they'd leave a lasting impression on her very pragmatic audience.

"A one-of-a-kind enterprise like this will fill a small but lucrative niche in the furniture market," she stated with confidence, clicking through slides of projections alternated with the most flattering photos from the property. "Barrett's Mill Furniture isn't a new venture, but rather the relaunch of an old, well-established business rooted in the Blue Ridge area. The product line will meet the desire of modern customers to feel connected to the nostalgia of days gone by. Backing this unique project would not only benefit Shenandoah Bank and Trust in the profit column, but gain us a valuable reputation as a firm that recognizes potential and invests in the future of our customers."

When she was finished, Chelsea set down the projector remote and took her seat midway down the polished conference table. Hoping to appear calm, she folded her hands in front of her upright tablet and waited.

Twelve pairs of eyes blinked at each other, roaming around the gathering but studiously avoiding her. Then, almost in unison, they all turned to the man seated in the place of honor at the head of the table. Her father was wearing a thoughtful expression, but from a lifetime of experience, she knew that didn't mean a thing. As a child, she'd quickly learned it was the normal, relaxed position of a handsome face that disguised a shrewd mind and gave away nothing.

As the silence stretched beyond thirty seconds, Theo Barnes let out a low chuckle. "Not all at once, now. We need to keep this civilized."

Nervous laughter flitted around the posh conference room, trailing off when he turned his dark eyes on her. At work, she wasn't his daughter, simply another bright employee charging her way up the corporate ladder, and he treated her accordingly. "You think this is a sound idea?"

Direct and precise, she reminded herself. He responded best to confident answers, even when he disagreed. "Yes, I do."

"And the numbers?"

"Bear me out, as you can see."

To prove her point, she pulled up the projection that showed Paul's business breaking even in two years and turning a profit within three. They were shaded toward the optimistic end of the spectrum, but having witnessed how committed he was to making the mill work, she had no doubt he'd find a way to honor his obligation to the bank. Nodding, her father swiveled his gaze around the committee, silently asking for their input.

"Chelsea, I have to say, I'm very impressed," said Alex Gordon, a good-looking colleague who dressed like a younger version of her father. Seated to his right in the heir-apparent chair that should have been hers, he gave her a smile that held more than a hint of personal admiration. "Your attention to detail is impeccable, as always."

"Thank you."

But you're not getting a third date, she added silently. Two had been more than enough, thank you very much. Her dad was convinced Alex was the financial genius of his generation, and in her saner moments, she acknowledged he was just the kind of man she was looking for. Polished and self-assured, he shared her interest in all things logical. There just wasn't a spark between them, at least not for her. Which was probably for the best, because as her father's hand-chosen protégé, Alex pushed every one of Chelsea's competitive buttons.

And she had a lot of them.

Now that the discussion had begun, one loan officer questioned her calculations, which Chelsea assured him were accurate. Another doubted the ability of such an out-of-the-way business to earn enough money to repay their loan. She patiently reminded him that the online component would minimize any disadvantage caused by the mill's remote location. On and on it went, and by the time they were done, she'd been pummeled for nearly half an hour.

"All right, then," her father announced as he checked his antique Swiss wristwatch. "Let's put this to rest. All in favor of approval?"

Chelsea's was the only hand that went up, and her heart sank to the floor. The formality of dissenting votes sealed it, and she fought to keep her disappointment from showing. She'd done her best, she reasoned as her father ended the meeting and stood. There was nothing more to be done. While she dreaded giving Paul the bad news, she felt something else she couldn't quite put her finger on.

Still puzzling over that, she gathered and stowed her things in her leather satchel. To her surprise, Dad caught her arm on his way by. "Walk with me, please. I have something to discuss with you."

It wasn't a question, and the way he phrased it left no room for refusal. She'd heard that kind of command many times while she was growing up but seldom at the office. What was going on?

When they arrived at his office, he ushered her inside and closed the door behind them. Turning to her, he got right to the point. "Are you certain the figure you named in your proposal will be enough to get this furniture business up and running and turning a profit?"

Chelsea was confused. Her numbers were based on Paul's, and she knew her father well enough to know he'd all but memorized anything with a dollar sign in front of it. "Are you looking for my personal guarantee that this company will make money?" After his curt nod, she sighed. "You know that's not possible. If I could do that, I'd be making a fortune on Wall Street."

Her attempt at humor got her nowhere, and he met it with a frown. "But you think it's a solid venture?"

"As solid as something like this can be." Since their exchange was strictly off-line, she decided to inject a little humanity into the equation. "You know as well as I do, the Barretts have never defaulted on anything. When they closed the mill, the ledgers were at zero, but they paid every creditor and former employee what they were owed. Paul's not the only one pushing this through. His family and the entire town are supporting this project. They're determined to make it work, and I think they have a real shot to do it. Even if they fail, they'll make sure the bank is repaid, no matter what."

Why she felt that confident, she couldn't really say. But that didn't matter in this situation. What counted was her conviction, and by the shifting mood on her father's features, she could see she was making progress. At this point in a negotiation with their president, she knew most of his staff would press on, trying to make their case even stronger. But she'd learned long ago that when the gears in his agile mind were turning, it was time to shut up and step back.

After what felt like an eternity, he nodded and strode across the plush Oriental rug to the focal point of his private domain: an original Monet set in a gilded frame. Turning to face her, he gave her a long, assessing look that told her absolutely nothing. When he finally spoke, she realized she'd been holding her breath and quietly let it out.

"This stays between you and me," he announced. "Based on your recommendation, I'm approving this venture on behalf of the bank. When the paperwork is complete, we'll deposit the amount you specified in the loan account, which is to be handled only by you. No one else—not even Paul Barrett—will have access to that money. You're to administer those funds as if they belong to me personally. Is that clear?"

Flabbergasted by his uncharacteristic behavior, she could only nod at first. Once she'd recovered enough to string coherent words together, she asked, "You've never gone against the loan committee before. Why are you doing it now?"

"It's a good investment."

She had the distinct feeling something unusual was going on, but she quelled her reservations because Paul needed this money to make Will's last few months happy ones. That it came with strings attached probably wouldn't matter to Paul, so she decided to simply be grateful. "You're right, and you won't regret making it."

"Definitely not, because I'm putting you in charge of making sure nothing goes wrong. Projects like this are notorious for exceeding both budget and deadlines. They need to be producing furniture by fall to meet the sales figures you've projected for the holiday season. You'll be on-site every day, ensuring things progress in a timely manner."

That wasn't part of Chelsea's plan, but the unyielding set of his jaw told her there was no wiggle room on this one. Either she oversaw the restoration, or it wouldn't happen. Paul was clearly accustomed to running his own life, and she feared that sharing control of anything with her wouldn't go over well. She didn't relish explaining the terms for his financing to him, but she'd figure something out. Maybe she could convince Will and Olivia to help her with that one.

"That's fine," she agreed. "I'll go out there a couple times a week to—"

"On-site, Chelsea," he repeated in that don't-argue-with-me tone that terrified everyone in his bank, from board members to tellers. "Every day."

"I have other accounts," she pointed out respectfully.

"Traveling four hours a day won't leave me time for anything else."

"Those clients will temporarily be reassigned. I'm sure Alex would be more than willing to take them all himself to impress me. And you," he added with a slight smile.

She didn't doubt that for a second. The idea of Alex filling in for her didn't sit well, but she couldn't come up with a good reason to protest. "All right. If that's what you want."

"It is. He's a very capable young man, and I've made no secret how I feel about him, on both a professional and personal level."

Not long ago she would've agreed with him, at least on principle. But today she viewed Alex in a different light, and it wasn't all that flattering. She couldn't put a finger on what had changed, so she couldn't explain it properly. Beyond that, she hated to disappoint the man who'd raised a teenage daughter on his own when the woman they'd both loved abandoned them.

So, like the dutiful child she'd always been, she nodded. "I appreciate you looking out for my best interests, Dad."

"Always," he assured her briskly. "As for housing, I'm sure you can find an acceptable place in Barrett's Mill. Because this is a personal request, I'll assume responsibility for your costs, of course."

Translation: *if you do this for me, I'll owe you a favor.*

It was the currency he traded in on a daily basis, to coerce people into doing what he wanted. In the end, he always got his way because no one had the guts to stand up to him and say no. That nagging whisper of warning grew louder, but Chelsea pointedly ignored it. He was the president of the bank, and although this arrangement was unconventional, it was the Barretts' only hope.

Not to mention her future vice presidency rested in his hands. If she went along, she'd be another step closer to her goal. If things went really well, she might even boot Alex from that coveted seat he'd charmed his way into. It was a win-win, so despite her lingering discomfort, she held out her hand. "We have a deal."

Chuckling, he accepted her gesture. "Of course we do. Now, if you'll excuse me, I'm running late for golf with the mayor. If I don't get there on time, he tees off without me and fudges on his score."

"Dad?" When he glanced back, she smiled. "Thank you for approving this project. I know it's a little outside the box, and I appreciate you giving it a chance."

Giving her a confident grin, he left her there to digest what had just happened. She and Paul had a big job ahead of them, but Chelsea couldn't help smiling. The next couple of months would be a lot of things, she mused as she made her way to her own office.

Boring wouldn't be one of them.

Wednesday morning started with a bang. Literally.

One of the temporary support beams Paul had set up to hold a set of pulleys chose today to slide out of place, and he barely leaped out of the way in time. Boyd, whose rough history had left him pretty much immune to catastrophes, bolted through the side door and raced toward the creek.

Paul couldn't blame him. Working alone so far from town had its downside, he decided while he coughed up decade-old sawdust and headed out to the porch for some fresh air. He caught the sound of tires crunching down the lane and was astonished to see Chelsea's convertible easing its way toward the mill. What was she doing back here? he wondered while he strolled out to meet her. At the most, he'd been expecting her to call sometime today to tell him his loan had been denied.

He figured she wouldn't come in person to deliver bad news, and his spirits lifted at the thought that somehow, despite everything stacked against him, he'd gotten the money he needed to reopen his family's business.

When she stepped from the car, Boyd galloped over to greet her, and she bent down to ruffle his big floppy ears. It was cute, and Paul couldn't help smiling as he approached. "He really likes you."

"He's a great dog," she agreed, straightening to look Paul in the eye. "I wanted to come and tell you in person that your loan was approved."

He'd suspected that, but hearing her say it made him grin like a fool. "That's amazing. What'd you say to them?"

After a moment's hesitation, she answered. "I presented my assessment and your estimate of what it would take to finish. The risk was deemed to be manageable, so you have your funding."

Her carefully worded spiel sounded awkward to him, but he chose not to question it. The important thing, he reminded himself, was that he could finish the rehab and bring the mill back up to working speed. "Well, whatever you did, I'm glad to have your help. Gram and Granddad will be thrilled, not to mention the rest of the town."

"That's good to hear," she said politely.

Her stiff attitude didn't do much to ease his vague concerns, but he had no idea how to broach the subject with her. He didn't want to borrow trouble, as his mother used to warn him about. Maybe Chelsea just wasn't a morning person. "So, what's next?"

"I have several documents for you to sign. And some conditions to discuss with you."

There it was, he thought as he swallowed a sigh. Like a trained dolphin who wanted a treat, he'd have to jump through some ridiculous hoop or other. Probably more than one. Muting his usual knee-jerk protest when someone tried to tell him how to do his job, he dredged up an agreeable smile. "I'm sure we can work it out. Come on in and we'll sort through everything."

Scrawling his name on the paperwork was the easy part. Once everything was completed in triplicate, Chelsea handed him his copy and stacked the others neatly in her briefcase before snapping it shut. This one was different from the one she'd brought the other day, with a zippered compartment he assumed held a slim laptop.

When it dawned on him that she'd brought her computer, the reason for her hesitance became crystal clear, and he bit back a groan. "You're gonna move in here and babysit me, aren't you?"

Her mouth dropped open, her eyes widening in shock. "How did you— Never mind," she added quickly, shaking her head. "You're right. I'll be here to make sure the project stays on time and on budget. You need to be producing stock by the beginning of September, which isn't that far away."

"I've never missed a deadline in my life," he retorted. "I've got no plans to start now."

"Plans go awry sometimes," she explained in a tone obviously meant to soothe his ego.

Her eyes shifted to the collapsed column, then back

to him, and angry as he was, he couldn't help chuckling. "That's structural, not financial."

"It's not your call," she said as she settled at the table and pulled out her computer. When she opened it, the machine greeted her with an upbeat chime, as if it couldn't wait to get to work. "I'm here to keep things on track until the project's finished. End of story."

That was what she thought. "You're gonna drive back and forth every day to stand over my shoulder and count how many nails I use? That's nuts."

Typing away, she replied, "Not that it should concern you, but I'm renting the Donaldsons' carriage house while I'm here."

How did he not know that? Paul wondered in bewilderment. Now that he thought about it, Gram had tried to tell him something that morning while he was laboring to get his truck started. Maybe he should've listened more closely instead of dismissing the local gossip as having nothing to do with him.

"In case you forgot, this isn't the safest place to be right now," he pointed out, feeling more desperate by the second. He didn't know why he was so adamant that she not be here, but he could only guess it was because this infuriating woman had so blithely invaded his domain. Not to mention charming his dog.

In response, she reached into a large bag and took out a regulation hard hat. Plunking it on her head, she gave him a triumphant smile and resumed tapping on her keyboard. He wasn't crazy about the prospect of her dogging his every move, but apparently that was how things were going to work. He'd known enough women to recognize when he was beat, so he gave up his pointless argument and decided to make the best of the situation.

Strolling into the office, he stood behind her to look over her shoulder. On the bright screen, he saw rows and rows of numbers, none of which made sense to him. The one thing he understood was that the red figures at the bottom were probably bad, and he frowned. "What's all this?"

"Your current cash flow." Pointing, she moved through columns until the totals finally turned black. "These are my projections based on your current situation and a reasonable estimate of your business leading up to the profitable holiday season. I always stay on the conservative side, so if things go well, the numbers could be even better."

Hearing optimism from this very businesslike woman made him grin. "I'll double 'em."

Expecting to be scolded for his brashness, he was pleasantly surprised when she returned his smile with a warm one of her own. "I hope so, Paul. Really, I do."

With that encouragement, she turned her attention back to whatever formula she was concocting, and he took that as his cue to leave her alone and headed for the door. Chancing a quick look back, he couldn't help noticing how the light caught the flecks of red in her hair and the fact that Boyd had returned and was now sprawled out under the table with his chin resting on the toes of her ivory shoes. Seeing as the bank insisted on having one of its bean counters ride herd over his business, at least they'd sent him one that was easy on the eyes.

Paul recognized it could be dangerous to be thinking that way about Chelsea. They went at everything from different angles, and working together day after day was likely to be a never-ending challenge for both of them. It would be best if they kept things strictly professional. Of course, that would be a lot easier if she didn't smell like a summer garden every time he walked by.

Her phone rang, and he couldn't miss the grimace on her face before she replaced it with a more positive expression. "Good morning, Alex. I'm just fine. How are you?"

Paul gave her a what's-up look, smothering a laugh as she rolled her eyes. Grabbing a pad and pen, he wrote, *Not-so-secret admirer?*

She nodded and he went to one knee, one hand over his heart and the other held out to her in a melodramatic plea. Shaking her head, she spun the chair away from him and finished the short, mostly one-way conversation. When she hung up, he couldn't resist yanking her chain a little. "Someone misses you, peaches."

"Don't call me that."

"Who is he? Not that I care or anything," he amended hastily so she wouldn't get the wrong idea. "Just wondering if some lovesick banker's gonna show up here and gum up the works."

"His name is Alex Gordon, and I doubt he could find this place with a GPS and a detailed map."

"Boyfriend?" It seemed unlikely given her reaction to his call, but Paul couldn't resist asking.

"Just a guy my father wants me to m—get to know better."

Interesting. "You were gonna say 'marry,' weren't you?"

"Yes," she breathed in a frustrated huff. "Alex is a Harvard MBA, from a good family, and he's in line for the same VP slot I've got my eye on."

"So you hate him."

"Of course not." He stared back at her, and she finally caved in with a faint smirk. "Okay, maybe a little."

"The same way you hated me in high school?"

"Go away."

She shooed him off and refocused on her data entry, and Paul got the message that she didn't want to discuss Alex. For some reason he was happy to hear she was single, though it shouldn't matter either way to him. He and Chelsea would work together for a few weeks, then part company. If she was in a relationship—or not—made no difference to him.

Putting those errant thoughts out of his head, Paul jammed the temporary beam back into place and secured it more tightly this time. His six-foot level told him it wasn't even close to being square, but that was nothing new. The whole place had been built more or less by eye, and he suspected the original crew had rolled a marble to determine how straight things were. But the resurrected building would have to pass a modern inspection, so it had to be done right. Even if that meant wrestling the off-kilter structure into compliance with his bare hands.

After plenty of measuring, sawing and drilling, the new support was in place, joined to the others with massive carriage bolts. Drenched in sweat, he stopped to wash the sawdust out of his throat. His large water bottle was empty, so he headed into the office to get another one from the fridge.

Boyd was gone, but Chelsea was immersed in something that was putting a troubling pucker between those stunning green eyes of hers. She didn't seem to hear him come in, so he paused in the doorway and made some noise to avoid startling her.

When she glanced up, the worry clouding her delicate features made him take a step back. "Something wrong?"

"We need to do an inventory," she replied in the kind

of tone usually reserved for reporters covering natural disasters.

The look that followed made it clear she expected him to respond with equal seriousness, but in his experience, no one had ever died from lack of counting stuff on a shelf. Especially considering the fact that the stuff on his shelves had been there for years, untouched and gathering dust. Who cared?

Since there didn't seem to be an actual emergency, he walked in and headed for the small fridge where her snappy briefcase was sitting. The elegant leather bag looked out of place in the rough-hewn office. *Much like its owner,* he thought with a grin. "When you say 'we,' you mean me, right?"

"I can help, but I'm not familiar with what you stock here. It'll probably go best if we do it together."

"And faster," he said, getting an urgent nod in reply. When the significance of that hit him, he groaned. "You wanna do it now, don't you?"

"I can't finish these forms until we know exactly what you've got on hand and how much it's worth. Depending on the value, it could make a difference in the valuation of the property. I did an estimate, but it needs to be confirmed with actual data."

"Because?"

"A higher value decreases the risk to the bank because they can sell the contents to help recoup their losses if you default on the loan."

"That won't happen," he insisted, motioning around him with the frosty bottle. "I won't let it."

"Of course not, but financial types need facts to support their decisions. As I'm sure you figured out when you applied to those other banks, everyone's nervous about lending money to new businesses these days. I'm just making sure we account for every dime of value this place has going for it."

She wasn't just saying that to appease him. He could see in her eyes that she truly believed those words. Knowing she had so much faith in him made his chest swell with pride. "I appreciate that. Since I don't have a clue what you just said, let me know what you need and I'll do my best to play along."

"I'm not playing," she informed him curtly, bringing to mind the prickly girl he'd known in high school. "I'm reinforcing. And trust me, you need every bit of it you can get."

The warm, fuzzy sensation he'd felt a few seconds ago evaporated into disdain. Being a follow-your-gut kind of guy, her devotion to numbers baffled him. "Why do you say that?"

Standing, she faced him squarely with the calm, cool demeanor he recalled from debate class. "Historical projects like this turn into quicksand like that." Snapping her fingers, she continued, "Termites, inferior engineering, whatever you can possibly think of goes wrong, and often you find problems no one even dreamed of. Before you know it, your budget doubles long before you finish, and a six-month project takes a year or more. I'm trying to guard against that happening to you."

To him, he echoed with curiosity. Not to the mill, but to him personally. Slight as it was, the deviation from her all-business attitude made him wonder if she was really as objective about all this as she claimed.

None of his concern, he cautioned himself as he took another swig of water and recapped the bottle. He'd treat this like their school assignments, working with her because he didn't have a choice. Two months wasn't all that long, he reasoned. Surely he could maneuver around her strict requirements until September. Then, once he'd proved the business was solid, she could go back to her office in Roanoke.

After returning his water to the fridge, he motioned toward the door. "The stockroom's in back. The sooner we get started, the sooner we'll be done."

"My thoughts exactly."

While she grabbed her tablet and plastic stylus, it dawned on Paul that they'd just agreed on something. Again. While the realization didn't settle well with him, he figured it'd make things easier if they were on the same page once in a while, so he let it slide.

He led her through the tomb and opened the new combination lock he'd put on the storage area. "There's some dangerous things in here, so I replaced the old padlock in case someone wandered in here after hours."

She gave him a shrewd look. "So the fact that you couldn't find the key had nothing to do with it?"

"Have I told you how much I missed that smart-aleck mouth of yours?"

"No."

"Huh." The tumblers clicked into place, and he slid the bar free of its metal loop. "Wonder why that is?"

From the corner of his eye, he caught her response and had to laugh. "Did you just stick your tongue out at me?"

"Oh, don't act so shocked," she informed him haughtily. "I'm sure you get that all the time."

Since she was right, he decided to give her this one. The door hung from a rusty track, and the wheels screeched in protest while he wrestled the solid oak panel open.

He snapped on the overhead lights, and she made a disapproving noise. "Was it always this bad?"

"Pretty much. Us Barretts are sawyers and carpenters, not interior decorators."

The small space was crammed to the gills with saw blades, a large assortment of mismatched tools and more than a few contraptions Granddad had made himself to maintain the sawmill. An entire rack was filled with boxes of various sizes. A few had labels, but most of them were a mystery.

Chelsea pinned him with a horrified look. "How do you know what's in here?"

"If I need something, I hunt around for a while. If it's not here, I don't have it." At first, he'd made a list as he went through each day, running by Stegall's Hardware on his way back into town at night. Then he'd run out of money, and by necessity he'd made do with what he had on hand. Since admitting that would make him sound pathetic, he kept it to himself.

Strolling across the dusty floor, she stood on tiptoe to see some of the hand-labeled items on an upper shelf. "Nails." Glancing at him, she actually smiled. "Seriously? Even I know there are lots of different kinds of nails. And how many are in there?"

Paul didn't like where this interrogation was heading, so he tried to derail her lecture with a shrug. "Got me."

"Let me get this straight," she continued in that rational tone he was beginning to hate. "You have to open all these boxes to find the right nails for whatever you're doing? That's incredibly inefficient."

"Well, it's just me here, so it's not that big a deal."

He finished with his most charming grin, but her skeptical expression made it clear she wasn't buying that.

Instead, she tapped her screen and brought up a digital list. "Now that I'm in charge, it *is* a big deal. We need to know what kind of nails and how many."

"In charge? Are you kidding me? You don't know the first thing about running a sawmill. I grew up here," he added, jabbing his finger into his chest for emphasis. "Not to mention I'm the owner. Not you."

After studying him for a few moments, she relented with a single dismissive nod. "Point taken, and I apologize. I meant that I'm handling the business end of things, at least for the time being. An inventory is part of that, and it needs to be done properly."

"Fine."

Her stylus poised to begin taking notes, she gave him an expectant look. He'd gotten himself into this mess by accepting her help, he realized. There was really nothing to do but go along with her demands.

Shoving his hands in his back pockets, Paul strode over to the shelf in question and began counting. "One, two, three—"

"Not a chance, hotshot. Are those boxes full or empty?"

"You want me to open each one?" Doing a quick scan, he glared at her. "There must be hundreds of 'em."

"The sooner you start, the sooner you'll be done."

Her sweet smile did nothing to disguise her mocking tone, and Paul crossed his arms in the stubborn pose that usually made people take a step back. "I'm not counting all these nails."

"You don't have to count each little one," she reasoned just as stubbornly. "If we fill a box with each variety and count those, we can calculate the rest."

Obsessive wasn't the word for what she was suggesting. In fact, he couldn't come up with a fitting description. Then he caught the flicker of uncertainty in her eyes, and suddenly it all made sense. Why she was here bird-dogging him. Why she was so insistent on dotting every last *i*.

"You're trying to impress your dad, aren't you?"

A slight tremor in her expression told him he'd hit that one dead-on, but she quickly masked it with coolness. "I don't see what that has to do with anything."

She hadn't denied it, which told him exactly what he needed to know. Each of them was being driven by family expectations, adding more pressure to an already stressful situation. If they didn't ease up on themselves—and each other—they'd both end up with ulcers.

Figuring it was up to him to defuse the tension, he said, "I need a break. Wanna take a walk?"

"But we haven't even started."

"This mess has been sitting here the last ten years." He dismissed it with a broad wave. "It'll wait another hour."

She glanced at her shoes, then met his gaze. "I'm not exactly dressed for a hike in the woods."

Spying a dusty pair of ladies' work boots on a shelf, he took them down and offered them to her. "These were Gram's, so they should fit you well enough."

Chelsea set down her tablet and reached for them before pulling her hands away. "There's nothing living in them, is there?"

Chuckling, Paul turned them upside down and banged on the bottoms to prove they were rodent-free. It struck him that her faint protest meant she was as ready for some fresh air as he was, and he congratulated himself on avoiding yet another wrangle with his old adversary.

Once she had them on, he angled his head to check out the effect. The cracked leather boots looked as odd with her classy suit as her high-tech computer equipment did in the office. But in the spirit of keeping the peace, he grinned. "It works for you."

"Just don't post any pictures online," she retorted as they headed for the side door. "My sorority sisters would never let me live it down."

He laughed, and after a few seconds, she joined in. It felt nice to share a joke with her that way. As they walked along the creek, he was careful to give her some space so she wouldn't feel as if he was crowding her. Even though he was a respectable distance away, he sensed her beginning to unwind a little, especially when she paused and took in a deep breath.

Smiling up at him, she said, "Much better."

Man, she was beautiful when she smiled. Especially out here, where the sun picked up the flecks of gold in her eyes. "That's good to hear."

They strolled along in companionable silence, the creek's steady current gurgling alongside them while birds chirped to each other in the trees overhead. Dappled sunlight filtered through the leafy branches, giving their path a jigsaw-puzzle look. Up ahead, he caught a motion in the brush and pulled Chelsea to a stop.

"Look," he said, pointing to a movement in the shadows.

A doe stepped from the tall grass, ears and nose twitching while she checked her surroundings for possible trouble. She stared right at Paul and Chelsea, her large brown eyes studying them warily. Apparently satisfied that they weren't a threat, she picked her way to the edge of the creek and lowered her head to drink. Behind her, two fawns cautiously followed her lead, flanking her in a stunning family picture Paul knew he wouldn't forget anytime soon.

When the deer had moved on, a solution to the inventory problem popped into his head. "Hey, I've got an idea."

Curiosity lit her eyes, and she gave him another, slightly different smile. "Really? What's that?"

"We buy those little bits and pieces by the pound. How 'bout if we box up each kind of nail, screw and whatsit and weigh 'em? Then we can put an accurate value on them for your inventory."

"*Our* inventory." Even though she corrected him, she sounded less bossy, so it didn't bother him as much this time. "That should work fine. Good idea, Paul."

For some reason, her praise made him stand a little taller. He told himself it was just knowing that he'd convinced the normally unmovable Chelsea Barnes to compromise. "Thanks."

They continued on to the end of the path, then turned around to return to the millhouse. They chatted about this and that all the way back, so the trip in was much more pleasant than the forced march he'd insisted on earlier.

Maybe, just maybe, this small success meant they could find a way to get through the next few weeks without killing each other. He sure hoped so, because against his better judgment, she was starting to grow on him.

Chapter Five

When she and Paul returned, Chelsea noticed Boyd curled up in the messy seating area on top of an old quilt.

"That's not his usual spot." Obviously concerned, Paul went over and hunkered down beside the bloodhound. "You okay, boy?"

Boyd thumped his tail but otherwise didn't move a muscle. Paul began checking him over, and when he got to the dog's huge right ear, he murmured, "Take a look at this."

Chelsea joined him and saw what had gotten his attention. A pale orange tiger kitten was curled up in a ball, sound asleep in its warm, furry cave. Next to the big hound, it looked small and helpless, and she knelt down to inspect it more closely. Apparently sensing the movement, the little cutie lifted its head and opened its eyes enough for her to see they were still blue.

Paul gently picked the cat up and did a quick survey. "Six weeks, I'd say, and a girl. Can't imagine where he found it."

As he returned the kitten to her spot, the thought that she might be one of several spurred Chelsea to her feet.

People could take care of themselves, but she had a very soft spot for tiny, vulnerable animals. "There could be more out in the woods somewhere. We should go look."

Patting his dog on the head, Paul stood and grinned at her. "What about your inventory?"

"That can wait," she retorted on her way to the door. "Are you coming?"

"Yes, ma'am." Still grinning, he grabbed an empty cardboard box marked *machine oil* and fell into step beside her.

They searched the tall grass around the mill, then moved farther into the woods in increasingly broader circles. They tramped carefully through the brush, moving branches aside, peeking into rabbit holes, anywhere a mama cat might think to hide her brood. While Chelsea made her way through the undergrowth, Paul walked the banks of the creek, keeping an eye out for paw prints they could follow. After more than an hour, they met back at the first bend in the stream, empty-handed.

"Boyd's not big on cars," Paul began, "so he usually sticks close to the mill when he goes wandering. He must have found it out here somewhere, but if there's any more, they're hidden really well."

"Did you see any tracks?"

"Not a one. It must have gotten away from the rest, and the mother gave up looking for it."

Spoken so matter-of-factly, his logical observation made Chelsea's eyes well with sympathy for the lost kitten. While she recognized that her parents' divorce had been inevitable, she'd never gotten over feeling abandoned by her own mother. When she was feeling morose, she couldn't help wondering how different her life would be now if she'd had a mom like everyone else.

Her prolonged silence must have gotten through to Paul, and he frowned. "I'm sorry for how that sounded, Chelsea. I wasn't thinking."

Blinking away tears, she summoned the polite smile she used so often to keep her emotions hidden from people. "That's okay, but I think we should get the kitten to a vet and make sure she's healthy. We don't want Boyd getting sick or anything."

Seemingly a step ahead of her, Paul crossed his arms with a chuckle. "Sounds like you think we're keeping that orange dust bunny."

Determined to save the little darling, she drew herself up to her full height, which was still no match for his. To compensate, she gave him the steely glare she'd perfected for use on obstinate corporate attorneys. "If you aren't, I am. But since Boyd brought her to you, I think he expects you to take care of her the way you did him."

That did it. The teasing glint left Paul's eyes, and he gave her a long, pensive look before nodding. "All right, she can stay."

"Oh, thank you!" she exclaimed, embracing him before she had a chance to think. When his arms settled lightly around her, the feeling of being so close to him was unlike anything she'd ever experienced. Thoroughly rattled, she quickly pulled away and took a healthy step back.

"You're welcome," he replied, a warm twinkle in his dark eyes. She wasn't sure if it was meant for her or his new guest, but she decided she'd be wise to ignore it. "How much can a scrap of fur like that eat, anyway?"

"The vet will know." Resisting the urge to tug at his hand, Chelsea began walking as fast as she could back to the mill.

"So we're going right now?" he called after her.

"I am," she hollered without looking back.

She heard him muttering behind her, but in a few strides he caught up. His long legs easily kept pace with her, and she found herself wondering how a guy who was so laid-back managed to get anything accomplished.

Despite the years that had passed, one thing hadn't changed: Paul Barrett made no sense to her whatsoever.

In the millhouse, Boyd was still standing—or rather lying—guard over his fuzzy charge. Chelsea carefully lifted the sleeping kitten and rewarded the hound with a thorough ear fluffing and a kiss between his big chocolate-colored eyes. "You're the best dog in the whole world, Boyd."

He responded with what could only be described as a canine smile, and behind her Paul laughed. "He seems to like you, too."

"You sound surprised," she commented as they made their way out to his truck.

"I am. Till now, I didn't think he had any taste at all."

The deftly angled flattery caught her off guard, and she gaped at him. "Did you just compliment me?"

"Actually, I complimented his taste in women," Paul pointed out, mischief glinting in his eyes. "But indirectly, I guess it says something nice about you. Two for one."

Bewildered by the shift in Paul's barely tolerant attitude toward her, Chelsea shook her head and climbed carefully into the front seat to avoid waking the kitten. Boyd came bounding from the millhouse and leaped into the back of the truck, sitting politely while Paul chuckled. "Guess he's coming along. Hope you don't mind."

"Of course not. He's my hero, not to mention hers," she added, nuzzling the soft bundle in her arms.

Slanting her an amused look, he didn't argue with her

for once. Chelsea appreciated the gesture, but she didn't know how to tell him so without inflating his already enormous ego, so she settled for a smile.

"Y'know, you have a great smile," he commented when the tires turned onto pavement.

It wasn't the first time he'd told her something like that, but it felt just as good this time around as it had before. "Thank you."

"I mean it," he continued as he maneuvered into the parking lot at the Mill Veterinary Clinic. "How come you don't bring it out more often?"

With a demanding career and absolutely no personal life, there wasn't a lot for her to smile about these days, but she wasn't about to tell him that. He'd feel sorry for her, and she couldn't bear that, not from him or anyone else. Given enough time, she firmly believed she was more than capable of wrestling her life into a better place.

That better place included a rambling house filled with kids and a big yard out back for the jungle gym and sandbox she'd longed for as a child. Maybe even a trampoline. Unfortunately, with her twenties ticking by and no future husband in sight, there were days when she feared she was running out of time.

Pushing aside her own troubles, she focused on getting inside without scaring the tiny cat in her arms. Fortunately, one of the vets was available, and after a quick examination he told Chelsea the stray was indeed a female about six weeks old.

"Most orange tigers are males," he added, gently rubbing a fingertip under the kitten's chin. "So this little girl is pretty special. Do you have a name yet?"

"Daisy" flew out of Chelsea's mouth before she had a chance to think, but it was perfect—her coloring was a blend of pale orange and white. Chelsea more calmly explained, "It's my favorite flower."

"Nice."

While the vet told her what her new friend needed to eat and drink, he kept a watchful eye on Daisy, who was sitting calmly on the metal exam table, staring up at Chelsea. The vet's focused attention grew more urgent, and Chelsea frowned. "Is something wrong?"

Without answering, he moved out of the cat's line of sight and said her name. She didn't react, and he said it again, more loudly this time. Chelsea thought he was being silly, since the kitten couldn't possibly recognize her name yet. When he clapped his hands a few times with the same nonresponse, she finally understood what he was doing.

"She's deaf," Chelsea murmured, tears stinging her eyes. She'd barely gotten acquainted with this baby, but knowing she couldn't hear anything made her unspeakably sad. "Do you think that's why the mother left her in the woods?"

"Could be. Animals have a way of knowing when something's wrong. Sometimes they'll care for damaged offspring, sometimes not."

Damaged.

The word hit Chelsea's chest like a hammer, and she struggled to mute the intense reaction into something more manageable. Analytical by nature, she approached everything in her life from a logical perspective. That this adorable creature should be doomed by a flaw completely out of her control seemed so unfair.

To Chelsea's astonishment, Paul came to Daisy's defense. "She's not damaged at all," he insisted, resting a hand on Chelsea's shoulder while he stroked the kitten's back. "She's her cute little self, and that's just fine. Isn't it, Daisy?"

Opening her mouth, she mewed up at him as if she agreed wholeheartedly, and the fist squeezing Chelsea's heart gradually released its grip.

"I'm sorry for how that must have come across to you," the vet apologized with a pained expression. "Working here, we see all kinds of things. We can sound too clinical sometimes."

Because he was sincere, Chelsea accepted his apology and moved on. "Do we need anything special to take care of a deaf cat?"

"Not really. But since she can't hear, she has to be an indoor pet. Other than that, just regular visits here and lots of love." Daisy nuzzled and licked his hand, and he chuckled. "She's a real sweetheart, so that shouldn't be a problem. I'll get some kitten formula and food for you to take home. Oh, and you should get a collar with a bell on it."

"But she can't hear it," Chelsea said.

"It's so you can hear her. She can get into lots of places, and she won't know you're calling her. It'll be tough to keep track of her if you don't know where she is."

"Thanks, Doc." Once the exam-room door closed, Paul gently grasped Chelsea by the shoulders and looked her straight in the eye. "Are you sure about this? We can find her a good home with someone else, if you want."

"I've never had a pet," Chelsea confided as she lifted Daisy and settled her into the crook of her arm. Leaning back, the dainty cat blinked up at her with a trusting look that settled the question right then and there. "But I've always wanted one. We'll figure it out, won't we, sweetie?"

"No doubt." Pulling open the door, he said, "I guess we have some shopping to do."

"Definitely. She needs something with a bell to wear and a litter box and a comfy bed to sleep in. And—"

She pulled up short when she saw Boyd already planted in front of the pet toys, eyeing them as if he were making his own list.

She traded a look with Paul, who shrugged. "Don't look at me. I don't understand him, either."

Laughing, she held Daisy up in front of the cat accessories to see if her new friend had a preference. She blinked in apparent confusion, and Chelsea laughed again. "I know. That's how I feel when I go shopping in Paris. Too many choices."

To narrow the selection a bit, she hooked three collars on her fingers, holding up one at a time. Daisy batted at a pink one with a silver bell that hung in the middle of an open heart rimmed in white rhinestones. While she knew the cat couldn't hear the noise, the sparkles obviously appealed to her, so Chelsea chose it and a similar one done up in lavender.

Paul gave her a you're-kidding look, and she explained, "A girl needs to have more than one of everything."

"Uh-huh." Following along, he watched in silence while she picked up several cat toys, balancing them in one hand and Daisy in the other. When she dropped a couple of things, he finally offered, "Would you like some help with those?"

"Yes, please."

Shaking his head, he picked up the ones on the floor and took the others from her. "You know she doesn't need all these, right? Most cats are happy with a Ping-Pong ball or some such thing."

"Daisy's going to be at work with me all day, so she'll need something to do." Around the corner, she stumbled on a display of crafts for animals. On a high peg, she spotted a quilted carrier with net sides and handles, done up in an adorable daisy print. Pointing, she asked, "Could you get that down for me, please?"

Paul obliged but had a question of his own. "Do you really think the mill office is a good place for a kitten?"

"I can't leave her alone at the carriage house for hours on end," Chelsea argued. "And the noise won't bother her, so she won't be scared when you fire up your power tools or the saws."

"Yeah, about that," he commented with a sigh. "I'm beginning to think I won't be able to hit our deadline on my own. If I'm gonna have the mill running in time to actually make furniture this fall, I need to hire some help."

"Did you have anyone in mind?" she asked while she pawed through a bin of squeaky toys shaped like everything from mice to birds. Even though Daisy wouldn't be able to pick up the noise they made, the bright colors and various textures might be fun for her.

"Some of the guys who used to work for Dad and Granddad are still around, and no one knows the equipment better than they do."

She picked up on an odd hitch in his usually confident voice and arched an eyebrow at him. "But?"

"Well, they're retired, so they won't want to mess up their finances by making too much extra money."

"Meaning you want to pay them in cash, under the table?"

Relief flooded his rugged features, and he grinned.

"I didn't think a by-the-book accountant like you would approve."

Time to nip this nonsense in the bud, she thought. In her sternest tone, she answered, "I don't, and neither will the bank. Everything Barrett's Mill Furniture does has to be completely aboveboard, or you'll have trouble with the IRS down the road. Anyone you hire needs to provide standard documentation, just like they would for any other job, and have all the proper withholdings taken out. Don't worry. I'll get the files set up for you and then show you how to do it."

"That sounds like a ton of work," he complained with a grimace. "Can't we just skip it for now?"

"No, we can't. That's the deal, take it or leave it." He still looked unconvinced, so she came up with an analogy he might actually accept. "I know you like to toss out the game plan and improvise, but if you want Shenandoah Bank's money, you have to play by the rules."

They stared at each other for a while, neither willing to concede defeat. In spite of the fact that it was making her life more difficult, Chelsea couldn't help admiring Paul's creative approach to solving problems. If he could just bring himself to bend that iron will of his on occasion, he'd make a fabulous executive.

When those dark eyes lightened a bit, she knew she'd made her point. "All right, fine. We'll do it your way."

The right way, she was dying to add, then thought better of it. She'd won this round, and there was nothing to be gained from rubbing his nose in it. Instinct warned her they'd have many more run-ins over the summer. It would be smart to keep some of her sharper weapons under wraps until she really needed them.

* * *

"So she's really staying, then?" Paul asked his grandmother at breakfast the next morning.

"Lila Donaldson told me Chelsea's renting the studio apartment in their carriage house month to month," Gram confirmed while she spooned scrambled eggs onto his plate. "Why?"

"No reason. Just curious."

Pausing, his grandmother gave him the eye. "You be nice to that girl, Paul. She's doing us a big favor with the bank, and we need that money."

"I know," he grumbled. "I wish it was someone else, that's all."

"Really?" Interest sparked in her eyes, and she sat down across from him. "Why is that?"

"She just bugs me. She always has."

"Hmm…I wonder why?"

Judging by the look she was giving him, she thought she had the answer all figured out. "Before you start planning one of your fix-ups, I'm not interested. I've got enough to do without worrying about some woman."

"We're not talking about some woman," she echoed with a smirk. "We're talking about Chelsea Barnes, one of the sweetest, smartest girls I've ever had the pleasure of meeting. Why you two never got along is beyond me."

"Molly thinks we're two stubborn mules pulling against each other."

"Maybe." She drew out the word as if considering it, then shook her head. "No, I think there's more to it than that."

"Don't even go there," he warned, pushing off from the table to stand. "Greg and Connor like being married, but being tied down isn't my style. And even if it was," he added before she could scold him, "I certainly wouldn't pick some sassy, tightly wound accountant."

"Sassy. I'd say that describes her perfectly."

"Got that right." Paul heard the frustration in his voice, and from the amused look his grandmother was giving him, he knew she'd caught it, too. "I didn't mean it as a compliment."

"Of course not, dear."

Her indulgent tone only added to his aggravation, and he reminded himself she was interfering out of love, not some perverse desire to drive him insane. Whistling for Boyd, he leaned in and kissed her cheek the way he had ever since he could remember. "Thanks for the eggs. Don't hold dinner for me, but tell Granddad I'll be home in time for the Braves' first pitch at seven."

"They're playing the Yankees tomorrow night, and the whole family's coming over for it. You should invite Chelsea if she's not busy," she added in an offhand manner clearly meant to suggest it wasn't a big deal to her.

Except he knew it was, and he didn't have the heart to disappoint this woman who'd doted on him his entire life. She'd been through a lot recently, and if attempting to match him up with Chelsea made her happy, he wasn't about to spoil her fun.

Pretending it was a huge concession, he gave in with a sigh. "Fine. I'll ask her."

"Good boy." Patting one cheek, she stood on tiptoe to kiss the other. "Have a good day."

That was the best part about being home again, Paul mused as he strolled out the door to his truck. When he left for work, there were people waiting at home to greet him, caring about what happened to him while he was gone. He'd lost a chunk of the independence he'd enjoyed for so long, but it was a good trade for the love he'd gotten in return.

Glancing over at his copilot, he said, "Cross your fingers, buddy."

The hound woofed in reply, and Paul turned the key in the ignition. After some sputtering, the engine churned to life and settled into a throaty rumble. It was after eight, and the small business district was buzzing. Obeying the speed limit of ten miles an hour, he had time to take in some of the everyday sights of his sleepy hometown. The parking spaces outside The Whistlestop were filled with cars, pickups and even a couple of tractors. As he drove past, he caught a whiff of hickory-smoked bacon and a blend of different kinds of coffee.

Bruce was setting the iron tables and chairs out front and stopped long enough to wave at Paul as he crept by. It was like that all the way down Main Street, and as he went, his mood steadily improved until he was smiling when he pulled in at the mill.

He was more than a little surprised to see Chelsea's silver car already in the turnaround. She didn't strike him as a morning person, so he couldn't imagine what had gotten a city girl like her moving so early. He trotted up the steps with Boyd close on his heels, and the sparkling front windows on either side of the door caught his eye.

"Hey, did you wash the—"

He abruptly stopped when he saw what she'd done with his wreck of a front room.

Everything was different. To his right, there was now a sunny sitting area, with a rustic bench under the wide window and a table on either side. Framed photos of the mill through the years hung on the walls, and two mismatched chairs flanked a braided throw rug that pulled it all together. On the other side, the scarred office furniture was arranged in an L, tucked into the corner opposite the Dutch door. That left space for Boyd's settee and a cabinet near the window. On top of that, a futuristic coffeemaker was brewing a cup of something that had a faintly nutty scent to it.

Glancing around for Chelsea, he found her on the floor holding Daisy in one arm while she mopped up water with a paper towel. "What happened?"

"Lila gave me some flowers for my desk, and while I was making coffee, Daisy started playing with them and knocked over the vase." Pausing, she gave him an accusing look. "It's going all over the place because this floor's not level."

"Tell me about it," he replied with a chuckle. Tearing off a wad of towels, he joined her on the floor.

While they sopped up the mess, he noticed the subtle floral pattern in her ivory blouse accented the vibrant color of her eyes, making them look even greener than they actually were. Or maybe it was the wispy curls that had escaped her ponytail to frame the delicate features he hadn't fully appreciated until this morning.

Startled by his new perspective, in self-defense, he stood and offered her a hand up. She was so independent he was stunned that she took it. But for some reason, knowing she'd allowed him to help her—just a little—made him smile. "I see you've been busy this morning."

"Just a few touches here and there. I hope you don't mind."

"Mind? It looks great. I'm a nuts-and-bolts kinda guy, so I don't pay much attention to decorating and such. I'm glad you do."

A pretty blush crept over her cheeks, and she cast her

eyes down to the kitten batting at her earring. "Thank you."

Her hushed response told him she wasn't accustomed to hearing praise, which made no sense to him. "Chelsea?" When she met his eyes, he gave her an encouraging smile. "I'm not one to blow smoke at people. If I tell you something, I mean it. You did a great job in here, and I'm really grateful."

"Okay." After a couple of seconds, she gave him a tentative smile. "Most guys tell me how nice I look and stop there. I guess I'm not used to getting recognition for what I do instead of how I look."

Beautiful as she was, Paul had no trouble believing that. But since she seemed so happy that he'd praised her accomplishments, he decided it was best to keep his admiring views on her looks to himself.

If he told her she was the prettiest thing he'd seen in months, she'd think he was just another one of those guys. He wanted Chelsea to know there was more to him than that. He just wasn't sure why.

"By the way," she continued, pointing to the small air conditioner humming in the window. "Did you come back last night to put that in?"

"Sure did. It gets pretty hot in there, and I didn't want you or your furry assistants melting."

"That's the most thoughtful thing anyone's ever done for me. Thank you."

As if that wasn't enough, she tacked on the most spectacular smile he'd ever seen in his life. He was fairly certain she'd gotten gifts way more expensive than his from guys who tooled around in upscale foreign cars, like the suit his ex had left him for. That memory still aggravated him, making Chelsea's gratitude all the more meaningful to him.

Despite what he'd told his grandmother, he suspected it wouldn't take much for Chelsea to get under his skin. Hoping to sound casual, he simply said, "You're welcome."

"I'd like to have a status meeting before you get started in back."

Just like that, the sweetheart was gone, leaving him with the stern taskmaster he secretly feared. "Now?"

"It'll only take a few minutes."

Grumbling under his breath, he took the printout she handed him before sprawling out on the settee. As he glanced over numbers that meant almost nothing to him, he finally latched on to the bottom line. "That stuff in the storeroom was worth how much?"

"It adds up," she agreed, plucking Daisy off the keyboard of her silver laptop to set her on the floor. Crumpling a piece of paper into a ball, she skipped it across the floor for the kitten to chase. "People often don't realize how much they've got till they account for it all."

Amazed by what had come of their seemingly endless counting, he grinned over at her. "And it's neat as a pin, besides, with those shelves all sorted and labeled like that. If it hadn't been for you, I'd still be tripping over boxes, trying to find what I'm looking for."

Her smile had a glint of pride in it, but she didn't chide him for doubting her. Instead, she went over to the coffeemaker and handed him a steaming mug of something that smelled like nuts and vanilla. "I'm glad you're pleased."

"Pleased? I'm totally psyched. You're an organizational genius." When she tipped her head with a suspicious look, he had to laugh. "Too much?"

She held her thumb and forefinger about an inch apart, but she was still smiling. While he listened, she mapped out what they needed to do businesswise, leaving him in charge of the production end of things. He went along with her suggestions because they made sense, and she didn't hassle him too much unless he floated an idea that was too far off the plan. Which, because he was himself, happened frequently.

The lady loved her spreadsheets, that was for sure, but he was surprised to find that her affinity for numbers complemented his more fluid style quite well. Except when they disagreed, and then it could get dicey. *Like now,* he thought as he heard a couple of cars pull up outside.

"Your reinforcements, I assume," she commented smugly. "Hank and Lila insisted I join them for breakfast up at their house this morning, and I heard all about the little chat you had with him last night. He's really excited about working here again."

"That's cool." When Paul had put out the call for help, it had actually felt awkward to be asking. It hadn't occurred to him that working part-time at the mill might be good for people who no longer had a lot to keep them occupied.

Apparently, Boyd's ears were as sharp as ever, and he was pacing in front of the Dutch door, anxious to greet their visitors. After making sure Daisy was safely in Chelsea's arms, Paul opened the door and closed it behind them as two older men tramped into the place where they'd worked for so many years.

Brothers-in-law Hank Donaldson and Joe Stegall had the well-worn look of men who'd spent a lot of time outside, putting in long hours at demanding jobs to make sure there was food on their families' tables. While they stood in the entryway looking around, he kept quiet to let them absorb the changes he and Chelsea had made.

The two traded a long stare, then turned to Paul in slow-motion unison. Their timing was dead-on, making him wonder if they'd practiced it beforehand.

"It'll do," Hank acknowledged with a stiff nod.

"Whatcha got in mind for us to be doin'?" Joe asked, his eyes narrowed. Paul didn't take that personally, since without the bifocals hanging from the cord around his neck, the man was blind as a bat.

"Good morning, gentlemen." Framed in the doorway, Chelsea gave them a queenly smile.

These two might not have been born in a mansion, but they'd been raised right. Both of them swept their grimy ball caps off their heads and returned her greeting.

"Would you like to have a seat while I get you some coffee?" she asked.

Apparently they hadn't been expecting the royal treatment, and Paul smothered a grin as he motioned them into the sunny sitting area. When she appeared with two mugs, they took them from her with approving nods.

Hank glanced around, and his face cracked into a rare smile for his pretty tenant. "Looks nice in here."

"Real homey," Joe agreed, slurping the gourmet blend she'd brewed. "Good coffee, too."

"There's plenty more, so don't be shy."

Daisy appeared behind Chelsea, stopping in her tracks when she saw they had company. To Paul's complete astonishment, the genetically gruff Hank leaned down and wiggled his fingers so she could see them. The kitten's eyes widened with excitement, and she lunged toward him, batting at his fingers, the laces of his scarred steel-toed boots, even the frayed cuffs on his pants.

"Yup, she's a real cutie," he approved, tapping her nose with a gentle touch completely at odds with his rough appearance. "We met the other night, and she took to me right off. I know how it is not to be able to hear so good, so we get along just fine."

Paul had known this man since he was a toddler, and he couldn't recall Hank ever stringing that many words together all at once. People would never cease to amaze him. The four of them chatted while they finished their coffee, and then he took the men on a tour so they'd have a sense of what they'd be getting themselves into if they signed up.

As they moved from the office into the hallway locker area, he felt his pulse spike as he was suddenly seized with an unfamiliar case of nerves. What if they thought he'd taken on more than even three men could handle? They hadn't commented on his idea of making furniture by hand or the wisdom of reopening a business that had been shuttered for ten years. Come to think of it, they hadn't said much beyond how nice the front room looked. It didn't bode well for what was coming next.

With his hand on the handle of the sliding door, he warned, "It's not pretty, but I think you'll get an idea of what I've got in mind."

"We're not here to judge you, son," Joe assured him with an encouraging wink. "Now, open the door and let's see what kinda mess you've made in there."

Taking a deep breath to steady his nerves, Paul yanked the rolling door to the side and let them walk in ahead of him. He didn't want to annoy them by hanging over their shoulders or trailing after them the way he had when he was a kid, asking question after question until they'd finally shooed him off with a few coins for a soda from the machine.

Where was that vintage dispenser, anyway? Paul wondered. It was nearly as old as Granddad, and if he could get it working again, it'd make a unique conversation piece for visitors. Listen to him, he thought with a grin. Chelsea's sermon about appealing to customers was already rubbing off on him.

"I've hit my limit," he confided while they examined his handiwork. "I could really use your help."

"When you called yesterday, you said you wanna make furniture the old-fashioned way." When Paul nodded, Joe looked perplexed. "Why?"

For what felt like the millionth time, he explained his idea to someone who clearly thought he was nuts. To his surprise, Hank humphed and said, "That oughta work. City folks love country things."

"They sure do," Paul agreed, thrilled to finally be speaking with someone who could follow his logic. He'd never have guessed it would be his grandfather's brusque foreman, but at this point he'd take any support he could get. "I'm hoping to have some rockers and benches ready in time for the holiday shopping season."

"These days, that's October," Joe pointed out with a scowl. "No way the three of us can do all that."

"Well, Jason's on his way here from Oregon. I haven't asked him, but he might be able to stay awhile and pitch in to get things running."

"Son, you could have a dozen brothers coming in from all over the map, wouldn't make no difference. For what you got in mind, in the time your granddaddy has left, you're gonna need more'n four of us."

He had a point, Paul recognized, and he decided to trust these two experienced pros. "How many more?"

The two put their balding heads together and muttered back and forth. When they were satisfied, Hank said, "Six off the old crew, two for the floor and four for carpentry."

"We'll be back with 'em Monday morning," Joe clarified.

Paul was astounded. These were men who'd left behind hard working lives and were enjoying their retirement. Then he realized he'd forgotten one very important detail. "I can't pay you guys much until we start making a profit."

They traded a look, and Hank said, "Then we'll do it for free."

"Seriously?" When they nodded, he pressed, "You really think they'll all come and work for nothing?"

Without hesitation, they spoke as if they were one person. "For Will."

A lump suddenly formed in his throat, and Paul swallowed hard to keep his emotions in check. On their own, they'd repeated the same vow he and Chelsea had made to each other, and hearing it from two of his grandfather's former employees emphasized how well loved and respected Will Barrett was in the town his family had built from the ground up.

Once he trusted himself to speak normally, Paul echoed them. "For Will."

Chapter Six

A delivery truck pulled up outside, and Chelsea met the driver on the front porch. Boyd wasn't happy about being barricaded in the office, so he jumped up on the settee and woofed his opinion through the window while Daisy blinked at the activity out front, her ears perked with curiosity.

Chuckling, the driver nodded toward them. "That's quite the pair you've got there."

"Yeah, they're something else." Eyeing the large box he held, she asked, "Is it heavy?"

He hefted it as though it were filled with feathers. "Not bad, but I can bring it in for you if you want."

"That'd be great. Thank you."

She propped open the door for him, and from out of nowhere, Paul appeared. Wiping his hands on a rag, he took the carton from the driver. "It's probably better if I take it from here. Hounds can be a little ornery about their space."

Boyd wasn't the least bit ornery, unless you counted him growling at the trio of red squirrels that raced across the porch every morning. Even then, Chelsea couldn't blame him, because she was convinced those rodents had no reason to do it other than to torture the poor bloodhound trapped inside.

Frowning at Paul's blatantly male display, she stepped past him and signed the driver's tablet. She handed him a tip and gave him her sweetest smile. "Thanks so much. Have a good day."

Grinning, he tipped his cap and sauntered back to his truck. When the door rolled shut and she was sure he couldn't hear anything inside the millhouse, she turned to glare at Paul.

The moron had the audacity to look baffled. "What?"

"That was incredibly rude. 'Hounds can be ornery about their space,'" she mocked. "What's the matter with you?"

"Just being on the safe side."

He said it with a completely straight face, and Chelsea waited for one of those aggravating grins. When it never surfaced, she realized he truly believed what he'd just told her.

It wasn't the first time a guy's behavior had bewildered her, she mused, and it probably wouldn't be the last. Since it wasn't that big a deal, she let it go and focused on her new purchase. "What do you think?"

Angling his head to look at the photo on the box, he said, "Looks like a tree covered in carpet."

"It's a playhouse for Daisy," Chelsea explained while she pried one end open. "She can sharpen her claws on it or climb on it, or hang out in the cubbies for a nap."

"This for the cat who prefers an old adding machine and paper roll to every toy you bought her at the vet's."

Chelsea had discovered that completely by accident when she was testing the archaic equipment to see if it still worked. Daisy had launched herself at it, obviously fascinated with the vibration of the dried-out printing mechanism and the motion of the paper. Because it wasn't good for anything else, it had become the kitten's favorite toy. Go figure.

"This is different," she argued, opening the Dutch door to drag the playhouse into her office. "She'll love it."

While the door was open, her mischievous pet dashed straight into the empty box. Scrambling around inside, Daisy lunged through the open end and back in, making so much noise Boyd came out to investigate. He quickly discovered he couldn't fit inside, but he sniffed at the pile of bubble wrap. Lying on top of it, he rolled around on his back, making the plastic squeak against the old floorboards.

"At least they like the box," Paul commented in a wry tone.

Making a face, she gave in to the animals' opinions and dragged the packaging into her office, cat and all. Boyd was close on her heels when the sound of a large truck rumbling down the lane detoured him from the office and to the screen door.

Through the window, she saw a long, high-sided flatbed filled with logs, easing its way down the rutted path toward the mill. When the horn echoed through the clearing, Boyd began howling, circling Paul's legs with an urgent let's-go kind of dance.

"Jason's here," Paul announced, opening the front door to let his dog race out ahead of him.

Chelsea remembered the youngest Barrett as a quiet boy whose two great loves were baseball and whittling. Now he was expertly maneuvering the biggest truck she'd ever seen onto a bridge scarcely wide enough to hold it.

How he managed that was beyond her, and she was impressed with how deftly he handled the mammoth load.

Paul directed him into the empty yard and motioned for him to park. When Jason stepped down from the cab, Boyd threw himself at the tall lumberjack, jumping and barking with such excitement he brought to mind a child greeting a favorite uncle. The two brothers embraced each other warmly, standing side by side as Chelsea joined them.

"What a great surprise!" Jason exclaimed with a swift hug for her. "Paul didn't tell me you'd be here."

For some reason, it irked her that Paul hadn't seen fit to mention her involvement in the project to his brother. After their conversation the other day, she'd assumed he shared her view that they were in this thing together. Clearly, he considered this a Barrett family endeavor, and her presence didn't merit any attention.

Putting aside her annoyance, she replied in her most syrupy voice, "Oh, he's been so busy it must've slipped his mind. How was your trip?"

"Fine. Long." Motioning toward the road with his thumb, he added, "I left Hobey sacked out at Mom and Dad's. He's getting some sleep, then taking the rig back in the morning."

Chelsea watched as understanding dawned in Paul's eyes. "You're staying?"

"You said you could use some more hands." Holding up two covered in scars, he grinned. "How 'bout these?"

Obviously astounded by the generous offer, Paul pulled his brother into a bear hug that would have crushed a smaller man. Grasping Jason by the shoulders, he held him at arm's length and simply said, "Thank you."

Chelsea still had trouble believing Paul was making

such a sacrifice for his grandfather. That Jason was following along made her a little misty, which was highly unprofessional. She was grateful they were too focused on each other to notice.

That didn't last long, though. Paul looked from Jason to her and said, "Since you're both here, Gram wanted me to invite you to the house tonight. The Braves are playing the Yankees, so everyone's coming over to watch the game."

It didn't escape Chelsea's notice that he was careful to make it clear Olivia had made the gesture herself. While she and Paul were hardly best friends, Chelsea had sensed a thawing of their old chill during the week and had assumed he felt the same way. Now she realized she'd been mistaken, and for some odd reason, it bothered her. A lot.

"Thanks, but it's been a long week," she said politely. "I think I'll just stay in tonight."

Paul looked as if she'd suggested flying to the moon that evening. "On a Friday night in the summer? You're kidding, right?"

His goading only made her angrier, and she struggled to keep her composure in front of his brother. "No, I'm not."

He traded a look with Jason, who smoothly said, "I'm kinda kinked up from the trip. Think I'll take a walk and stretch my legs."

Boyd's sharp ears picked up on the walk comment and he loped over to follow Jason out to the creek path Paul had cleared. When they were out of earshot, Paul turned to her with a frown. "Something wrong?"

"Of course not."

Holding her gaze for a couple of intense seconds, he shook his head. "I've done this before, y'know. That's the kind of look a woman puts on when she's mad at me but doesn't want to talk about it."

She didn't appreciate being lumped in with the other women he'd known, but there was no way she was sharing that with him. "I have no idea what you're talking about."

"Right." He dragged that out in a skeptical drawl, then understanding glimmered in his eyes. "I didn't ask you right, did I?" When she didn't respond, he sighed. "I should've made it clear we'd all like to have you there tonight. I thought if I asked you, you'd say no. I'm sorry."

That he'd so quickly identified the problem was impressive, to say the least. Maybe the macho athlete she'd known in high school had actually become more sensitive over the years. She was pretty sure stranger things had happened, but she couldn't come up with any examples just then.

Since he appeared genuinely sorry, she decided to give him a break. "Apology accepted. Can I bring anything for the party?"

"Just yourself. Mom, Gram and my sisters-in-law are handling everything else." His relieved smile wavered a bit. "You won't tell 'em I blew the invitation thing, will you?"

"Just this once," she teased. "But don't let it happen again."

"Yes, ma'am."

Loud whistling sounded from in back of the mill, an obvious attempt to let them know Jason was on his way back.

Trading smiles with Paul, she said, "His timing is pretty good. Did he used to bug you and your dates in high school?"

Paul groaned. "All the time. It wasn't just me, though. He did it to all of us."

"So he's had a lot of practice," she commented as Jason trotted up the porch steps.

"Too much." Turning to his brother, Paul asked, "Ready to unload?"

Glancing around, Jason frowned. "It's just the two of us?"

"And Chelsea."

Eyeing the mountain of logs braced in the truck, she shook her head. "I'm not going anywhere near that."

Paul gave her a cajoling look, and she answered with a glare of her own. They stared at each other for a few seconds, neither willing to give an inch. Finally, his face broke into a *gotcha* kind of smirk. "I'm just yankin' your chain. None of us is gonna be on the ground while we unload."

Of course not, she realized, feeling foolish that she'd even briefly considered it a possibility. Jason didn't say anything, but she noticed him shaking his head at them. She'd gotten accustomed to haggling with Paul over every little thing, and she barely noticed it anymore. In fact, she kind of enjoyed sparring with him, but she could only imagine what Jason thought of their antics.

She stood on the porch, watching while the Barretts checked over the clamps holding the huge logs in place on either side of the oversize truck. When they were satisfied, Paul took some kind of remote box from the cab and retreated to stand beside her. Once Jason and Boyd had joined them, Paul did another visual sweep of the yard and nodded. "Okay, here we go."

"You sure you remember how to use that thing?" Jason needled like the irksome little brother she recalled from their childhood. Only now he loomed even larger than Paul and didn't shrink from the scowl he got in reply. Instead, he raised his eyebrows in an innocent expression that made Paul grin.

"Watch me."

With an expert touch on the controls, he fired up the crane mounted on the truck and lifted out the first log. It settled on the ground with barely a shiver, and she doubted he could do it again. But he did. Over and over, one at a time, until the entire payload was stacked in a neat pyramid of nineteenth-century oak. It was a remarkable feat, and while she wasn't one to gush, she decided it called for some praise.

Applauding the effort, she said, "Very nice. I wouldn't have thought anyone could stack all that wood without wrecking something."

"That's nothing," Paul told her as he powered off the remote. "Wait till you see us strip the bark and rip the logs into lumber for the saws. That's something you won't want to miss."

He pointed at what appeared to be an outdoor version of the mill saws. The big difference was there was nothing around it, so they could slide in as big a tree as they wanted and guide it through the nasty-looking blade that stood taller than her. The sight of it reminded her of those old movies where the damsel in distress was headed toward certain death and rescued by the hero just in time.

That image led to another, more pragmatic one, and she wondered if they'd go for it. Only one way to find out, she decided, so she charged ahead. "Hey, I've got kind of a kooky idea."

Jason groaned, but Paul cushioned his reaction with

an indulgent smile. "No, she's good at this. Go ahead, Chelsea."

The compliment, quick but honest, thrilled her. All week, they'd been competing in a kind of tug-of-war, both of them motivated by their determination to do the best possible job they could. That Paul had noticed her contributions—and appreciated them—touched her in a way she experienced so rarely she could tally them on one hand.

Buoyed by his support, she outlined her brainstorm. "We could invite people out here to watch you guys work. Most people have only read about lumberjacks, so it would be something new for them to see it for real."

"You mean like a carnival or something?" Jason asked.

"More like a picnic for local residents who remember this as a working mill," she clarified, glancing at Paul to gauge his opinion. His face told her nothing, but curiosity glimmered in his dark eyes, and she took that as a good sign. "We could do it as part of a grand reopening to announce the business is up and running again. We'd show people how you're bringing this place back to life, and they'll feel like they're a part of it."

"While we're at it, Jason and I could fell some trees," Paul suggested, nodding out toward the overgrown lane. "We've gotta do something about widening that access road anyway. Might as well make it part of the show."

His response was more or less a stamp of approval on her idea, but Chelsea wasn't one for assumptions. They got you into trouble, and she preferred to have official sign-off before she got too excited about something. "Does that mean you're on board?"

"Sure." Looking at his brother, he asked, "How 'bout you?"

"Why not? It'll be fun. Once we get some trees down, maybe we can do some logrolling in the creek."

Chelsea wasn't sure about that one. "I've seen that on TV, and it looks pretty dangerous."

"Only if you're Paul," Jason retorted with a laugh. "Every time we do it, he ends up in the drink."

"That's 'cause you cheat," he snarled, his grin making it clear he didn't really mind the ribbing all that much.

"I don't have to, since you're *so* bad at it."

"We'll just see about that."

Hooking his younger brother around the neck, Paul angled him away to inspect their precious load of hundred-year-old timber. As they strolled off, still harassing each other mercilessly, Chelsea shook her head and went back inside.

At least in there, it would be quiet.

When Paul and Boyd pulled in, the old homestead was lit up like a hotel. Cars and pickups were parked up and down the tree-lined street, and he noticed a few neighbors hiking over on foot. Apparently the family gathering had morphed into an all-out party, Barrett-style.

Perfect, he thought with a grin. This was what Gram and Granddad wanted, to enjoy his last few months on earth. He crammed his truck into a narrow opening beside the garage and caught his buddy's collar before opening the door. "You can beg, but no stealing off people's plates. Got it?"

Boyd gave him one of those morose hound-dog looks, but he woofed in agreement, so Paul let him go and opened the door. Boyd was off like a shot, and Paul hoped he'd behave himself. Folks stood around the spacious backyard, chatting in groups while four grills made enough smoke and mouthwatering scents to bring in guests from all over town.

Bruce Harkness was manning his portable smoker, trading gibes with anyone who approached him with an empty plate. Paul's father, Tom, was flipping burgers on one grill while big brothers Greg and Connor were coaching a gaggle of kids in a chaotic Wiffle ball game in the side yard. Some genius had mounted Granddad's huge flat-screen TV to the side of the garden shed, and dozens of lawn chairs were set up, ready for the pregame festivities.

Chelsea's picnic idea for the mill popped into his head, and Paul couldn't keep back a smile. Apparently, the very disciplined accountant had a flair for public relations. It was enough to make a guy wonder what other talents might be lurking behind those sparkling green eyes.

As if on cue from some unseen director, her convertible slowed out on the street, doubling back to take a spot a considerable distance from the house. Since this was his family's bash, Paul figured he ought to be a good host and go greet her.

As he strolled up the sidewalk, he had to admit he was eager to find out how they'd fare with each other away from their odd working situation. They'd been more or less thrown together, and the first week had gone as well as could be expected for two people who saw everything from completely opposite angles.

Not that it mattered, he assured himself as he approached her car. Once the mill project was done, she'd go her way and he'd go his. But the remainder of that time would pass more smoothly if they could find a way to continue getting along.

Waiting for her to get out, he offered a welcoming smile. "Hey, there. Glad you could make it."

She flashed him one of those amazing smiles that would knock him off his stride if he wasn't careful. "From the look of things, this is the party of the year. I wouldn't miss it for anything." Pressing the button to pop the trunk, she lifted out a couple of gallon jugs of sweet tea. "I picked these up on my way, but they won't be nearly enough. Should I go back and get more?"

"Nah, we've got plenty."

Her bright expression faltered into a frown. "How stupid of me. Your mom and Olivia must make their own, and it's probably way better than this. I wanted to bring something, and I couldn't think of anything else."

"It wasn't stupid. It was a thoughtful thing to do, and we appreciate it." Adding a smile, he was pleased to see hers come back. He began walking toward the fun. "Where's your furry roommate tonight?"

"The Donaldsons adore her, so she's hanging out with them." Laughing, she said, "I'm still flabbergasted by how much Hank dotes on her. He never struck me as an animal person."

"Folks change as they get older. I know I have."

She slanted him a curious look, then gave him another, softer smile. "I guess we both have."

Hoping to continue this warmer version of their usual banter, he said, "For the better."

That made her laugh, which had been his intent. Still, the carefree sound caught him off guard, and he felt an odd sensation deep in his chest. Fortunately, they'd arrived at the house, so he didn't have a chance to ponder it any further. He'd learned that with women, when you examined things too closely, it could only lead to trouble.

Something told him he'd have to watch his step with the new-and-improved Chelsea, or he'd wind up in over his head in no time flat.

They hadn't gotten two steps inside the yard before the kitchen door banged open and Gram came rushing onto the side porch. Normally she was calm and dignified, so her uncharacteristic exit worried him until he saw the delighted look on her face.

"Chelsea!" Pulling her into a hug, Gram set her away, still beaming. "How wonderful of you to come. We know how busy you and Paul have been out at the mill."

He picked up on the not-so-subtle way she connected their names, and by the amused look on her face, so did Chelsea. She didn't seem to mind, and he was surprised to find he didn't, either. He must be more tired than he thought.

"I wouldn't be anywhere else tonight," she replied in a fond tone. "This place is like a ghost town. Now I know it's because everyone's here."

Like the gracious Southern lady she was, Gram waved away the compliment. "Oh, just a little get-together for our friends. The Braves are playing the Yankees, you know."

Chelsea slid him a glance, eyes twinkling in fun. "It seems like I heard that somewhere."

"There's some folks here you haven't met," Gram said, linking an arm through their guest's. "Give those to Paul, and I'll introduce you to the girls in the kitchen."

Taking that as his dismissal, he pretended to grumble but followed them into the house with a light step. From what he'd seen so far, this little shindig was a raging success.

Then he got a look at his grandmother's kitchen.

It was a huge room, but chaos seemed to have taken over the normally orderly space. The flurry of female activity and voices, blended with the mix of various perfumes, would have been too much for a lot of men. But Paul resolutely held his ground, waiting for his mother to notice him.

Born and raised in nearby Cambridge, Diane Barrett had always divided her time between her husband's family in Barrett's Mill and her own. She was the kind of person who took care of things, whether that meant raising her own five sons or caring for the countless kids who moved through the church teen centers she'd founded in both towns.

"Chelsea!" she exclaimed, folding her into one of her famous hugs. "How have you been?"

"Good, thanks." Glancing around, she laughed. "It looks like you could use some help in here."

"This is nothing. You should see it during the holidays." When she glanced up and saw Paul, her cheeks dimpled with the welcoming smile that always greeted him when he came home from wherever he'd been. "There's my boy. There should be room for those in the second fridge on the back porch."

"Gotcha."

"When you're done with that, I've got another job for you."

Her matter-of-fact tone made it clear it wasn't a tough one, so Paul unloaded the tea and returned for his next assignment.

"I wish we'd had that teen center when I was growing up," Chelsea was saying. "It must be nice for those kids to have a place to go instead of home to an empty house."

"For some of them, it's a real godsend," Mom agreed

while she mixed macaroni salad in a tub large enough to wash a baby in. "Olivia used to enjoy coming in and mixing with the kids, but it's harder for her to do that now."

"I send snacks in with Paul," she added with a wistful smile. "I do miss seeing everyone, though."

This was the first he'd heard of it, and it hit him that she never left the house anymore. Caring for Granddad consumed every waking hour of her day. "I'll stay with Granddad so you can go down there, Gram. Just tell me when."

"Thank you, honey. I'll let you know."

But he knew she wouldn't. Watching her unwrap plasticware to set in a large pan, he wished there was something he could do to help the stubborn, loving woman who'd adored him from the moment he was born. Even though she wasn't sick herself, she was hurting in a way no one should have to endure. A problem solver by nature, he wasn't used to feeling helpless.

"You okay?" Chelsea murmured, rubbing his shoulder.

He nearly brushed her off, until he caught the sympathy in her eyes. They'd spent a lot of time together the past few days, and she'd become more attuned to his feelings than most of the women he'd dated. Frowning, he shook his head. "Not really, but thanks for asking."

"I'll think of a way to get her in to see the kids," Chelsea promised. "I think it would really do her some good."

"She won't leave Granddad."

That got him a sly smile and a wink. "Then I'll come up with some other way to get her a break. I'm good with details."

Having seen her in action, he didn't doubt she'd find a way to make good on her promise. As she sauntered away to join the crew making hamburgers, his mother popped in to take her place. Very quietly, she said, “Will needs some help getting outside, but he won’t let your dad or Jason do it.”

“And you’re thinking he’ll go along if I ask him, is that it?” When she nodded hopefully, he chuckled. “Do I look like Houdini?”

“Oh, you’ll think of something,” she answered breezily. “Maybe Chelsea will have an idea.”

“She’s got plenty of those,” he muttered, “but none of ’em are gonna do me any good with Granddad.”

“Then I guess you’ll have to figure it out on your own. Thanks, honey.”

Patting his cheek, she hustled off as one of the women shrieked her name. After confirming the crisis wasn’t fire related, Paul left the kitchen and went around the house up to the front porch steps. By the time he got there, he had a plan, and he whistled for Boyd.

His reliable buddy came bounding up to him, and Paul stopped him with a hand in the air. “Be quiet and wait here, okay?”

Seeming to sense something was up, the dog obediently sat and wagged his long tail. As a rule, Paul couldn’t say for certain that the dog actually understood him, but this time he couldn’t explain it any other way. Leaving Boyd on the porch, he entered the dining room, leaving the screen door ajar behind him.

“Hey, Granddad,” he said easily, looking around the large room. “Have you seen Boyd?”

Wearing a Braves jersey and cap, Will was sitting in a straight-backed chair, obviously trying to catch his breath after hauling himself out of bed. When he simply shook his head, Paul’s heart lurched in a way he knew he’d never get used to. It hurt him to see his strong, stoic grandfather reduced to such a weak state, but he got a firm grip on his emotions so they wouldn't show. For Will, the worst thing anyone could do was feel sorry for him.

So Paul resolutely charged ahead. "There's so many people here, I'm afraid he'll get trampled. Could you help me look for him?"

The thought of a dog being harmed got Granddad's attention, and he straightened up in the chair. "Of course. Just give me a minute."

"That's great. Thanks."

Paul began whistling, and right on cue, Boyd came trotting into the house, a telltale smear of mustard on his nose. He bumped Paul's knee, then sat politely in front of Granddad.

"Hey, here he is." Keeping up the ruse, he patted the dog's head. "How was your snack?"

Woofing, he rolled his tongue out of his mouth in approval of the food, making them both laugh.

"I had a dog like you when I was a boy," Granddad commented with a nostalgic smile. "We named him Casey, because Casey Stengel was our favorite baseball player."

"I remember you telling us about that old hound. He's buried out back, right?"

"Under a sugar maple tree. He liked to roll in honeysuckle, so we planted that bush out there for him." His eyes misted a bit, then cleared when they met Paul's. "I know your mother sent you in here to help me outside, so let's get it over with. Just make it look good, all right?"

"How 'bout we carry one of those coolers sitting on the front porch? You hold the handle on one side and lean on me. I'll do the rest." His grandfather thanked him in a faint voice, and Paul summoned an encouraging smile.

"No problem. You used to carry me when I was little. Now it's my turn."

"You're a good boy," Granddad told him in a rough voice. "Don't ever let anyone tell you different."

"Don't worry," Paul assured him with a grin. "I don't."

That got him a watery laugh, and he waited while his grandfather collected himself. When he gave a firm nod, Paul put an arm around his back and got him steady on his feet. The cooler trick probably didn't fool anyone, and when they showed up in the backyard with it, folks casually gave them a little extra room to pass by.

Leaving it with the other drinks, Granddad made the few steps to his front-row seat on his own. It was a Braves director's chair with *Barrett* embroidered on the back, and once he was seated, Boyd ambled over to settle down beside him like a furry guard.

What a great dog, Paul thought as he went down the line putting together plates of food for the two of them. Of course, the fact that Boyd could count on Granddad sneaking him some food probably had something to do with his devotion.

When Paul ran into Chelsea at the dessert table, she smiled at him. "Mission accomplished, I see."

He chuckled. "Boyd and I made it work."

Leaning closer, she murmured, "Helping someone without making them feel helpless is a real art. Good for you."

The comment made his chest swell with pride, and he couldn't keep back a grin. "Thanks." Then, without him realizing it, he heard himself ask, "Would you like to join us?"

He had no idea what had possessed him to say that, but it was too late to take it back now. From her shocked expression, Chelsea was just as stunned by the invitation as he was.

She recovered quickly, though, and rewarded him with one of her beautiful smiles. “That would be nice.”

Relieved by her response, he grinned down at her. “Yeah, it would.”

“Are we agreeing?” she teased, mischief dancing in her eyes. “Again?”

Groaning, he replied, “Aw, man. I must be more tired than I thought.”

“That or I’m wearing you down,” she tossed back as they made their way to their seats.

On TV, a small band was playing the national anthem, and they stood until the song was over. While they got comfortable in their lawn chairs, the last thing she’d said echoed in Paul’s head, and he did his best to shake it free.

Because if the beautiful and very intelligent Chelsea Barnes was beginning to wear him down, he was in big, big trouble.

Chapter Seven

Chelsea spent most of Saturday running errands she'd been putting off while she got settled into her new position at the mill. So when Sunday morning rolled around, she was content to lounge in bed with Daisy purring next to her, listening to the quiet.

Her rental cottage was tucked in behind the Donaldsons' main house, which blocked most of the noise from the street. Because of that, the only sounds she heard were birds chattering back and forth to each other from the trees and the occasional bark of a neighbor's dog. It was a huge departure from the bustling nature of Roanoke, and it didn't take her long to realize she liked it better. A lot better.

Her hometown had always seemed *too* quiet, she mused while she stroked between the kitten's perky ears. Her younger self had been eager to break free and see the world. Now that she had, she could appreciate the appeal of a slower pace that gave people time to enjoy things instead of rushing past them on their way somewhere else. She couldn't imagine living here full-time, of course, but now that she'd accepted her circumstances, she was looking forward to spending the summer in Barrett's Mill.

The bells of the Crossroads Church chimed nine, and in the middle of a yawn, a stray thought entered her mind: she should go to church. It had been ages, but after the warm receptions she'd been getting all over town, she had no doubt Pastor Griggs would welcome her at his Sunday service.

Inspired, she shifted Daisy onto the other pillow and got up. Clearly unconcerned, her tiny roommate curled into a ball and promptly went back to sleep.

"At least I won't have to worry about you missing me too much," Chelsea murmured on her way into the bathroom. In the interest of time, instead of blow-drying, she spiraled her damp hair into a French twist and put on a summery dress and flats.

By the time she headed out the door, her landlords were coming down their steps. She met them on the sidewalk with a smile. "Good morning. Mind if I join you?"

"Not a bit," Lila assured her, and they began a leisurely stroll toward the other end of the street. They met up with several others doing the same, and by the time she reached the little white chapel, Chelsea was pretty well caught up on the happenings around town. Working out at the mill, so far from the center of things, she was woefully out of touch, and she paid close attention to the latest news.

"Ran off with her daughter's boyfriend," Fred Morgan's wife, Helen, finished in a shocked tone. "The scandal of it would kill me, let me tell you."

Chelsea hadn't caught who had done the running off, but another muted conversation floated in, and she registered the name as being one of her high school teachers.

Scandal was the right word, for sure, she acknowledged with a grin.

"Now, Helen," Fred chided her. "You don't know that for a fact."

"I sure do. I saw them myself, racing out of town in his sports car like their tails were on fire."

Shaking his head, Fred asked Chelsea, "Speaking of cars, how's that little monster of yours running these days?"

"Never better. You haven't lost your touch."

"Well, now, that's good to know."

Then, completely out of the blue, Ginny Thorndike asked, "Chelsea, how are things going with you and Paul?"

The question hit her like a bolt of lightning, and she knew she had about two seconds to come up with a response before these well-meaning biddies assumed they'd hit a nerve. And began spreading the word that Chelsea had gotten tongue-tied over a simple question about Paul Barrett.

"It's going well," she replied as casually as she could manage. "Now that Jason and some of the other mill employees will be helping out, things should really start moving along."

Ginny traded a look with Lila, who gave her a slight shrug. Never one to be easily put off, Ginny tried again. "I meant, how is it working with Paul? If memory serves, you two never got along."

That was putting it mildly, but Chelsea had anticipated the follow-up, so this time she was prepared. "True, but that was way back in high school. We're grown-up now, and we've got a job to do, so we're making it work."

"Are you going to the reunion?" Helen asked as they

approached the church. "Brenda told me it's later this month."

Brenda Morgan had been in their small graduating class, but Chelsea was so far out of touch with things, the reunion was news to her. Now that she thought about it, though, it had been ten years, so it was time for some kind of get-together. "I guess I can, since I'm here. Who should I call for details?"

"Brenda's in charge of it," Helen said proudly. "She and her husband will be at church with the kids, so you can ask her then."

Chelsea recalled her old classmate, a perky redhead with dark, sparkling eyes and a figure to die for. Every guy in school had chased after her, and every once in a while she'd let one of them catch her. Chelsea had a tough time picturing her as a responsible adult, and she wondered how much the wife and mother resembled the teenager Brenda had once been.

When they connected in the vestibule, Helen reintroduced them, and it was obvious Brenda hadn't changed a bit. Bubbly as ever, she was surrounded by four children who appeared to range in age from eight to a few months. Squealing with delight, she shifted the infant to one hip in a practiced motion and reached out to embrace Chelsea.

"It's so awesome to see you!" Leaning closer, she murmured, "I hear you've got your hands full with Paul Barrett these days. If you need any help, let me know."

She added a wink, and her husband laughed. "I think you've got enough to do without adding him to the list. Steve Lattimore," he added, offering his hand to Chelsea.

"It's nice to meet you," she replied, glancing around the circle of children. "All of you."

Brenda rattled off their names, but with the buzz of

conversation in the background, Chelsea didn't quite catch them. If she was pressed later on, she'd have to fess up, she supposed, but for now, she settled for "They're great, Brenda. You must be very proud."

"Most days," she said with a giggle. "Others, not so much. You know what I mean."

Not really, Chelsea thought, but she decided not to go there. "I should probably go find a seat."

She turned and ran smack into the broadest, hardest chest she'd ever encountered. Tilting her head back, she met up with Paul's twinkling brown eyes. "I've got one saved for you up front, if you want it."

"Hello, Paul," Brenda cooed, batting her eyelashes shamelessly. Apparently Steve was well acquainted with his wife's flirtatious nature, because he greeted Paul with a grin and a handshake.

"I've got a great idea!" Brenda went on. "Since you're both in town, you can lead the first dance at the reunion. You know, our top two graduates together again, that kind of thing."

The look on Paul's face was a humorous blend of shock and horror, and Chelsea couldn't resist teasing him. "What's the matter, Paul? Is the thought of dancing with me really that bad?"

Meeting her gaze head-on, he gave her one of those slow, maddening grins. "As long as you let me lead, it should go fine."

A couple of awkward seconds passed, and they continued staring at each other, each waiting for the other to give in. Finally, Chelsea ended their standoff with a laugh. "Fine. You can lead, but I get to pick the song."

"Deal."

They shook on it, and Brenda let out a melodramatic

sigh. "Whew! For a minute there, I was afraid we'd have to step in between you."

"Are you two always like that?" Steve asked.

"Like what?" Chelsea and Paul responded in unison, and they all laughed.

"'The more things change, the more they stay the same,'" Brenda quoted, gathering her brood together. "I'll get the reunion info to you later, Chelsea. If you have time, we'd love to get you on the committee. There's a million things to do, and we could really use someone who's organized and efficient. If you're interested, our next meeting is at seven tonight at Arabesque."

"What's that?"

"It used to be Morgan's Dance Studio," she explained. "My cousin Amy just moved here, and she's taken over the business from Aunt Helen. Wait till you see what she's done with the place."

Chelsea found their choice of venue odd, to say the least. "Why do you meet there?"

"It's big, quiet and there are no kids," Brenda replied, ticking its attributes off on her fingers. "We get a lot done, then we get a chance to chat before heading home to put our rug rats to bed. I'm actually going to miss it when the reunion's over," she added with a wistful sigh.

She made it sound like fun, but Chelsea was still wary. "Who's working on it with you?"

She rattled off the Friday-night roster of the old cheerleading squad. In high school, they'd had nothing whatsoever to do with her, Chelsea recalled with more than a little attitude. They must be desperate for more members to share the load. Then again, reconnecting with Paul had gone well, erasing years of bad teenage memories for her. While she was normally cautious when it came to people, her success with him made her more willing to take another leap. If she gave these women a chance, it just might lead to the same positive result. At the very worst, they'd remain the nodding acquaintances they'd always been. No harm done. "I'd be happy to help. Do you need my number?"

"Aunt Lila has it. I'll just get it from her."

As the Lattimores headed inside, Chelsea shook her head at Paul. "I forgot how tightly connected this place is."

"Yeah, it's kinda nice," he said, lightly touching her back to guide her toward the open sanctuary doors. "Folks look out for each other."

"It *is* nice," she agreed as they walked up the far aisle. When they reached the end of the pew, she turned to look back at him. "I forgot to tell you I had a great time at the picnic Friday night. Thanks for inviting me."

"You're welcome." His expression held a genuine warmth she hadn't seen before. Just as quickly as it sprang up, though, it morphed into a smirk. "It was fun having you there, even if you don't know squat about baseball."

Fortunately for him, the organist began playing the opening chords of "Just a Closer Walk with Thee," so she didn't have time to work up a crushing reply. But she'd get him later, she vowed as she opened her hymnal, and it would be a doozy.

While they sang, she let her gaze wander a bit, admiring the humble church with an adult's perspective. Constructed in 1866 of lumber from the mill, the church had solid oak beams supporting the roof that had darkened with age and decades of oil-lamp smoke. Tall windows ran along each of the side walls, letting in sunbeams that spotlighted different people in the congregation as fluffy clouds moved through the sky outside. Behind the altar hung an oil painting of Jesus addressing a gathering of worshippers, his arms outstretched in a loving gesture that included them all.

From the corner of her eye, she noticed a flurry of movement down the row, and she glanced over to find Diane Barrett waving to get her attention. Holding her thumb and pinkie like a phone, she mouthed, "Call me."

Chelsea had no clue what that might be about, but she nodded anyway. If she was able to help out with something, she'd do what she could. In Roanoke, she didn't have much personal time, and she guarded it like the treasure it was. Being here let her slow her customary pace, giving her a chance to sit back and enjoy things rather than planning what came next. It was a pleasant change. She felt Paul shift beside her to whisper, "What's up with you and Mom?"

Keeping her attention on the pastor's opening prayer, she shushed him.

Unfortunately, that only made him chuckle. "Did you just shush me?"

"Yes," she hissed. "Now be quiet and behave yourself."

With another chuckle, he said, "Yes, ma'am," then sat back in his seat.

Since they had only one book between them, her respite didn't last long. When they stood for the next song, he moved closer so they could both see. Close enough for her to register the warmth of his skin through his button-down shirt, the reassuring feel of him standing beside her.

That was how he'd be with the woman who finally tamed that wild heart of his, Chelsea knew. Strong and solid, allowing her to be who she was but standing nearby in case she needed him. Because that was the kind of man he'd grown into, and when he finally found someone to settle down with, she'd be the center of his world.

Her thoughts had drifted so far afield she was startled to realize the music had stopped. Rattled by her complete lack of concentration, she put an end to her romantic nonsense and focused on the pastor's sermon on the importance of family.

"Here, we join our own families—" he swept a hand through the air to encompass everyone "—with the larger one God has made for us. In this community, we find the love and understanding we need to make the good times better and the tough times a little easier. Some of us may wander away," he added with a fatherly smile, "but we can always come back, confident that our Heavenly Father and His faithful will be here waiting for us."

People throughout the congregation were nodding, and to her surprise, Chelsea found herself doing the same. Because that was how she felt, she realized with sudden clarity, how she'd felt since that first day when she and Paul had lunch at The Whistlestop. She'd been gone a long time, but the residents of Barrett's Mill had not only acknowledged her return, they'd embraced it.

This morning, she'd come to a place she'd avoided for years simply because she'd rather sleep than pray. Folks had been there to greet her, easing the awkwardness she'd feared, and God Himself had rewarded her effort with open arms, welcoming her back to His house as if she'd never left.

Sitting in this country chapel filled with sunlight and joy, she felt more at ease than she had in a very long time. That wasn't a coincidence, she knew, and she looked up to heaven with a grateful smile.

It was good to be home.

* * *

Chelsea pulled up in front of the dance studio a few minutes before seven. She still had reservations about joining a group she'd been excluded from as a teenager, and she figured arriving first would give her time to settle her nerves before the others got here. It was a balmy night, so she had the top down on her car and some mellow country ballads on her playlist. Resting her head against the seat, she stared up at the first few winking stars, enjoying the quiet. It was a Sunday kind of peace, and it struck her that the calm she'd experienced in church this morning had followed her through the rest of her day. Sending a smile heavenward, she sighed. "Thank You."

A puff of breeze warmed her cheek, and even her pragmatic mind couldn't deny it felt as though someone had brushed a gentle touch over her skin. The door of the building opened, and she swiveled her head to find a slender woman in capris and a fluttery-sleeve top approaching her convertible. Chelsea wasn't that tall herself, but the new dance teacher was tiny by comparison.

"Are you okay?" she asked with obvious concern.

"Just fine," Chelsea assured her, offering a hand. "Chelsea Barnes. I'm helping out the reunion committee, but I'm a little early, so I thought it'd be less annoying for you if I waited out here."

Her grip was surprisingly firm for someone so petite. "Amy Morgan, and you're welcome to wait inside. Brenda dropped off some snacks earlier, and I'm just doing the books, so you won't bother me."

"Okay." Leaving the car, she tried to come up with something to start a conversation. "You're Brenda's cousin, right?"

Amy nodded. "I was born here, but Mom and I moved

away when I was six. Aunt Helen's been having trouble keeping up with the kids and was thinking of closing the studio, so I came to keep things running for her."

"That was nice of you." As Amy reached for the old-fashioned door, Chelsea stopped in her tracks. The inset was beveled, with a ballerina in a graceful pose etched into the glass. Above it in an elegant arch was the word *Arabesque,* done in a flowing script that looked perfect over the dancer. "This is absolutely gorgeous."

"Isn't it, though? My friend Jenna Reed is an artist, and when I told her what I wanted, she came up with this."

"Molly Harkness said she did the sign for The Whistlestop," Chelsea commented as they went inside. "I've been meaning to contact her about new signage for the mill, but I misplaced the contact information Molly gave me." In truth, Paul was the one who'd lost it, but she didn't think Amy would care about that.

"I've got her info right here." Pulling a slim phone from her front pocket, she said, "What's your email?"

Chelsea rattled it off, and in the span of a few seconds, they'd exchanged not only Jenna's details, but their own. As Chelsea glanced around, she saw that the front area was mostly open, with plenty of space for floor seating in front of an elevated stage. Her one and only tap class had ended badly twenty years ago, and she hadn't been back since. But Brenda had said Amy was making major changes to the old building, so she felt safe in saying, "This place looks great."

She got a shy smile for her trouble. "Thanks. Uncle Fred helps out when he can, but his own business comes first. The velvet curtains are out being repaired, but when they're rehung they'll really help bring things together."

"Definitely." Hoping to draw Amy out a little by discussing her business, Chelsea asked, "So, how many students do you have?"

"Fourteen right now, but I'm always looking for more if you know anyone."

Inspiration struck, and she suggested, "Have you tried the teen center at the church? They offer before- and after-school care for younger children, too. You might find some customers there."

Amy's mouth had tightened at the word *church,* but she quickly masked her negative reaction. "I'd hate to bother the pastor. He must be very busy."

"He's not in charge of it. Diane Barrett is. I can introduce you to her, if you like."

"Thanks. I'll let you know," she said as the front door swung open and a gaggle of former cheerleaders swarmed inside. After a quick wave at her cousin, Amy vanished into her office so quickly it was almost as if she'd never been there at all.

Timid by nature, Chelsea understood her withdrawal from the sudden commotion all too well. Turning to face a herd of girls who'd baffled her throughout high school, she almost wished she could trail after Amy and skip the meeting. But she'd given Brenda her word, so she braced herself and went to greet the committee. After a lot of squealing and unexpected hugs, she felt much better about the whole thing. Something about bygones being bygones, she presumed. Well, if they could manage it, so could she.

Once everyone had something to nibble on, they settled around a large round table and got started. Chelsea had brought her tablet, and Stacy Harrington leaned in with great interest. "Ooh, look at that! The picture's so clear it's like looking out a window."

Feeling generous, Chelsea took out her stylus and offered them both to her. Stacy's eyes nearly popped out of her head. "Are you sure?"

"I'm not much of a note taker, so go ahead."

After a few quick pointers, Stacy had the hang of it and rewarded Chelsea with a huge smile. "Oh, this is fun. I've been saving up for one, but my minivan needs a new transmission..."

She trailed off with a sigh, and Chelsea almost felt guilty. She'd popped into the store at the mall one day and walked out with the latest, greatest gadget she could find. "You're welcome to use it at our meetings if you want."

"That'd be fabulous! Thank you."

"No problem."

While she explored the various apps, they chatted back and forth about nothing in particular. Then Stacy leaned in to speak more privately. "You know, when Brenda said you were joining us, I wasn't sure about it. You're nothing like I remember from high school. No offense," she added hastily.

Chelsea laughed quietly. "None taken. I guess we've all grown up since then."

"Most of us, anyway," Stacy replied with a giggle. "Paul Barrett hasn't changed one tiny bit, God bless him."

For some odd reason, her assessment made Chelsea want to defend him. Thinking again, she decided against it. If it got around that she was singing his praises, folks would jump to all kinds of conclusions that would only complicate both of their lives. So as difficult as it was to let the misimpression stand, she reluctantly did just that.

The business portion of the meeting lasted about half

an hour, giving way to the kind of hen session she'd always gone to great lengths to avoid. Tonight, though, she was more or less trapped, so she listened politely to the other women's lively discussion of men, diapers and how to keep a Crock-Pot roast tender while it cooked all day long.

Not long ago, she'd have scoffed at such mundane conversation as being boring and unimportant. But sitting here with them, she gained an appreciation for her former classmates' busy but simple lives. Married to their high school sweethearts, they were navigating the twists and turns of modern life, raising their children along the way. Normally she was content with the choice she'd made to focus on her career and delay having a family until it made more sense for her.

But tonight, for the first time, she felt a trickle of doubt creeping into her well-laid plans. Why it had chosen now to appear, she couldn't begin to explain, but she didn't like it. Not one bit.

When Paul pulled in at the mill, he had to look twice to be sure he wasn't seeing things. There were several pickups parked next to Chelsea's car, and through his open window he caught the scent of fresh coffee and snippets of laughing conversation. Excited by the prospect of company, Boyd scratched on his door until Paul leaned over to pop the handle for him. The hound made a beeline for the open front door, and Paul wished he could match the dog's enthusiasm.

Since starting this project, he'd been praying for God to send him some extra hands. Well, now he had them. The problem was, he wasn't sure what to do with them, and he wished he had Chelsea's flair for planning and organization. If he did, he'd be rushing inside like Boyd instead of dragging his feet every step of the way.

He paused on the porch, searching for a way to go in without looking as though he was making an entrance. When Chelsea spotted him, she flashed him a bright, encouraging smile that made all his doubts fade into the background.

"Morning, boss," she said easily. "Would you like some coffee?"

Taking the mug she offered him, he muttered, "Please don't call me that."

Sympathy flooded her eyes, but it was quickly replaced by determination. "Someone has to be in charge, Paul. For better or worse, it's you. Deal with it."

Taken aback by the harsh comment, he growled, "You learn that from your dad?"

"Among other things." Now the smile was back, and she patted his arm. "If you need me, I'll be in my office trying to find a pen."

"You bought a dozen of 'em on Friday." Then he figured it out and laughed. "Let me guess. Daisy hid them on you."

"The office isn't that big. I can't imagine where she hides them all."

Grinning, he reached into the back pocket of his jeans and fished out a beat-up ballpoint. "Just don't let your furry assistant get at it. It's the only one I've got."

"Thank you."

Beaming her appreciation, she tucked the pen behind her ear. Paul followed the motion for some reason, and he noticed she wasn't wearing her usual earrings. "No diamonds today?"

Casting a look at the little crowd in the entryway,

she shook her head. "They don't seem appropriate for this job."

He was impressed that she'd considered how other people would view her fancy clothes and jewelry. Now that he got another look at her, he saw she'd played down everything, from her plain watch to her flat shoes. Even her hair, which was pulled back with a simple band instead of yanked into some fancy do most folks would see only on TV. Now, instead of resembling an executive in some cushy office, she looked like a regular person. A very pretty one.

Since she'd made such an effort, he decided it wouldn't hurt to share his opinion. "I like this look better anyway. It's more you."

"Really?" Apparently, the response had popped out on its own, because she narrowed her eyes at him. "You're razzing me, aren't you?"

"Not a bit." Her dubious frown made him want to rush in and reassure her, but he suspected she'd push away any attempt to make her feel better. Instead, he sipped his coffee and casually said, "I appreciate you making the place look so nice for the crew."

The compliment included redecorating the lobby as well as her appearance, and from her dawning smile, she realized that. She was sharp, he reminded himself for the hundredth time. But for once it didn't bother him. In fact, now that he'd gotten used to her directness, he liked it. Maybe just a little too much.

Before he could make a mess of their working relationship, he finished off his coffee and set the mug on a nearby table. Picking up the bag he'd brought in with him, he said, "Well, we'd best get to work. It's bound to get noisy, so I brought you these."

When she pulled out the sound-canceling headphones, you'd have thought he'd brought her the crown jewels. "You bought these for me?"

"Standard issue at a sawmill," he explained. "We've all got 'em."

Gazing up at him, she gave him a look he couldn't begin to describe. All he knew was it made him want to squirm. "You could've just told me to get some."

"I figured this was easier, since I know what kind of rating you need."

"That was very sweet of you, Paul." Stepping in, she quickly kissed his cheek. "Thank you."

The spot her lips touched warmed instantly, and he felt the heat spreading with the grin that was taking over his face without his permission. "You're welcome."

Touching his arm, she passed by in a cloud of summery scent that filled his head with soft, feminine sensations that had no place in his image of Chelsea. They were partners in this project, he reminded himself sternly. The restoration of the mill meant too much to his grandfather for Paul to lose sight of the end zone when he'd finally assembled the team they needed to push across the goal line.

With that in mind, he shoved the brief encounter with Chelsea aside and turned to face his crew. They were eyeing him strangely, and Jason—idiot that he was—was making no attempt to disguise his curiosity.

"Nice perks, being the boss and all," he teased, eyes crinkling in fun. "Is that part of the benefits plan?"

"Not for you."

When Paul registered the snarl in his voice, he did his best to laugh it off. His entire life, he'd never had a rival for a woman's attention. Not that his younger brother was a threat or anything, seeing as Paul wasn't interested in Chelsea that way to begin with.

A couple of the older guys were chuckling to each other, and he decided it was best to nip their suspicions in the bud before they had a chance to mention them to their wives. Because once that happened, the incredibly efficient Barrett's Mill gossip chain would make mincemeat of him.

"All right, fun's over. We're all here to do a job, whether it's in the mill or the office," he stressed. "Hank, you were our last foreman, and I'd appreciate you taking that on again."

The man acknowledged the request with a single nod, but the pride shining in his eyes told Paul he'd made the right decision. "You all know what to do to get this place running like a top, so I'll leave you to it. I don't want you pushing yourselves too hard in this heat, so make sure you take a break once in a while. Any questions, I'll be out clearing trees with Jason."

"You can count on us, boss," Joe promised.

Paul would prefer not to be referred to that way, but Chelsea's words rang in his mind, and he forced a smile. "I never doubted that, but it's good to hear."

With that, he snagged his troublemaking little brother around the throat and dragged him out front for some one-on-one chain-saw time.

When they'd reached the woods, Jason stopped and set his chain saw down. "So, you wanna tell me what's really going on?"

"With what?"

"You and Chelsea." Paul was so stunned by his brother's perceptiveness, he didn't know how to respond.

"She's really getting to you, isn't she?" Jason pressed.

For a second, Paul debated playing dumb, then decided against it. Jason knew him better than anyone, and claiming ignorance would only delay the inevitable. "If you mean she's driving me over the edge, then yes. I thought Mom and Gram were bad, but Chelsea's the most stubborn, frustrating woman I've ever met in my life."

"You forgot smart," Jason goaded. "I mean, that's what's really bugging you, right?"

Much as he hated to admit it, Jason had nailed the real problem dead-on. Jamming his hands in his pockets, he sighed. "I've dated some really beautiful women, but none of 'em could think their way out of a paper bag. Chelsea could tell you how it was made and figure out a way to make you want to buy one. The trouble is…"

When he trailed off, Jason filled in the blank for him. "The trouble is, she's going back to Roanoke soon, so you don't have much time to make a move."

The urge to shove his brother back a few steps was almost overwhelming, but they were adults now, and at work besides. So Paul settled for a stern glare. "That's not funny."

"Wow," Jason said somberly. "You must really like her."

Paul suspected he was losing his mind, because the last thing he'd ever envisioned himself doing was asking anyone for advice on women. Then again, he wasn't doing a bang-up job on his own. He'd been working side by side with Chelsea every day, and he hadn't found the guts to tell her how he was feeling. Maybe, he mused with a frown, that was because he wasn't exactly sure himself.

"I guess you're right," he muttered. "Whattya think I should do?"

After thinking a few seconds, Jason snapped his fingers. "Ask her to the reunion. You're both going anyway, so you can make it sound like just two friends driving in together. Then see what happens."

"That's not half-bad," Paul acknowledged, feeling a hopeful spark flare inside him. "Thanks."

"Anytime."

Patting his shoulder, Jason fired up his chain saw and headed for one of the trees they'd marked for felling. Given the chance to reconsider his plan, Paul was stunned to find he didn't want to. Oh, man, he groaned silently. Was he in trouble now.

Before long, Chelsea had her new routine down pat. Paul was an early starter, but since Daisy woke her up before the neighbor's rooster, she managed to get in half an hour earlier than he did and have some kind of breakfast laid out for his volunteer crew. Even though she saw proof of it every day, she still couldn't believe they were all willing to put in so many hours of hard work for free.

Raised by a man who could run a complete return-on-investment assessment in his head, offering something so valuable for nothing was a foreign concept to her. But she had to admit they really knew what they were doing, and they deserved some tangible recognition of their labor. Even if it was just doughnuts and coffee.

Sitting down with her morning tea, she opened her email to find a message from Brenda Lattimore.

Final count: 82. Need more chairs :(

Chelsea typed back, No problem, then added an uncharacteristic smiley face.

Most of her email was completely professional, but spending so much time with the outgoing Brenda and her chatty committee had given her a new perspective on the girls she'd viewed with such disdain in high school. Thanks to them, now she could see how her lonely teenage existence had been partly her own fault. Maybe if she'd made more of an effort to fit in with her classmates instead of looking down on them, she would've had more friends.

Since she couldn't go back and change her past, Chelsea had resolved to make her present more fun. Paul was an excellent role model for that, although she couldn't envision herself ever being quite that laid-back. Still, there was always room for improvement, and she saw no harm in trying. For instance, she no longer checked her schedule a dozen times a day to make sure she was on track. Instead, she kept her to-do list short enough to memorize. It made life much easier.

Sipping her tea, she looked around with a satisfied smile. *Rustic* hadn't been the word for this place when she'd first arrived. Now the machinery hummed as if it had never been off-line, and people came and went with a regularity that would have been unthinkable when she did her initial site appraisal for the bank. It was a vibrant, interesting place, just the kind of spot folks would enjoy visiting for a few hours with their kids.

With that in mind, she opened the website she was designing and reviewed her progress. After a few false starts, she'd gotten the hang of the program and had the basics in place.

One thing she didn't like: the company logo. Paul wanted to use the wood-burning mark they put on their lumber, but it struck her as being too much like a brand cowboys used on cattle. The problem was, some long-ago Barrett had created it, and it would be a nice historical link between the original mill and its modern counterpart.

She now had a solution to that, she thought, pulling up Jenna's number on her contact list. When the artist answered, the grinding noise in the background nearly drowned her out. "Hello? Can you hear me?"

"Yes."

"I think we've got a bad connection."

"No, it's my deburring machine. What can I do for you?"

Since the woman didn't seem inclined to shut the equipment off, Chelsea went on. "Amy Morgan and Molly Harkness recommended you to do some artwork for the sawmill. Are you taking on new projects these days?"

"Every day," she replied with a laugh. "What did you have in mind?"

By the time Chelsea had finished outlining what she wanted, she was almost hoarse from shouting. But Jenna seemed totally unfazed by both the racket and the assignment, promising she'd have some drawings in a couple of days. "Email whatever visuals you have, and I'll take it from there. 'Bye."

Chelsea wasn't sure her goodbye got through, but she ended the call and pulled up the primitive graphics files she'd scanned and saved to her laptop. She'd just hit Send when she noticed Paul on the other side of the Dutch door, wearing a curious look and a dusting of powdered sugar from a leftover doughnut.

"I could hear all that from out in the shop. Are your ears okay?"

Playing along, she cupped her ear. "What?"

"Did you just make a joke?" he asked, his jaw open in mock surprise.

At least, she hoped it was. She'd hate to think she was so serious he believed she was incapable of making a simple joke. Judging by his grin, he was just ribbing her, and she relaxed. "I hired Jenna Reed to design our new signage and a banner for the website, so I was going over a few things with her."

"Great idea. Everyone's gone for lunch, so it's just us. Can I see what you've got so far?"

Normally Chelsea didn't share anything that wasn't absolutely perfect. But this was Paul's business, not hers, and while she wasn't thrilled with showing him an incomplete product, she couldn't come up with a good reason not to. "Sure. Come on in."

Peering over the door, he made sure Daisy wasn't underfoot before pushing it open. Chelsea had to admit she loved how gently he treated her little friend. He hadn't even blinked when she'd mentioned bringing Daisy to work, and he frequently played with her during his breaks. Then he'd take Boyd out for a run and bring the hound back worn-out and ready for a nap on the settee. Where Paul found that kind of energy baffled her, and she'd come to admire his seemingly endless stamina.

He stood behind her, listening as she clicked through various areas of the site and explained how they'd work. She nutshelled her concept for their new logo, using the Barrett's Mill brand as part of the design. The plan was to use it on everything from the roadside sign to mugs and caps they'd sell online and in their gift shop.

"Granddad will be thrilled with that idea. I'm glad you thought of it."

Spinning in her chair, she faced him squarely. "This is the first time you've seen any of this. Don't you want to make some changes?"

He shrugged. "You're way better at that kinda stuff than I am. Even if I thought your idea was kooky, I'd have gone with it 'cause you know what catches people's eyes. But Granddad likes the old mark, so I appreciate you coming up with a way to use it. It's a good compromise."

Come to think of it, they'd been doing a lot of that during their partnership. While he read the history page, Chelsea reflected on those first difficult days, when they'd each been jockeying for position, trying to convince the other to see things their way. There was no denying things had changed between them, but when? And more important, how?

She and Paul were the two most headstrong people she knew, but somehow they'd found ways to overcome their stubbornness and work together. Maybe, she mused with a smile, how it had come to be wasn't important. What mattered was keeping it going until the project was finished.

And then what?

Her optimism faltered, and she busied herself straightening up her desk so Paul wouldn't pick up on her shifting emotions. Unlike most men she'd known, he noticed things like that, and she didn't want to be forced to come up with a plausible explanation for it. A quick peek showed her he was focused on the website and not on her, which was a relief.

The problem was, she couldn't ignore the way her stomach dropped every time she considered leaving sleepy Barrett's Mill and returning to her demanding job in Roanoke. Here people valued her input and respected her opinion even if they didn't necessarily agree with her. At the bank, she often felt that no matter how many hours she put in, they weren't enough. Or her pace wasn't fast enough, or any number of other flaws she wasn't even aware of.

Did she really want to go back to that? she wondered, wiggling a pencil while Daisy batted at the eraser. And if she didn't, what on earth would she do instead?

"You ever think of doing this kinda thing professionally?"

Paul's question jerked her out of her own head. When she realized he'd somehow picked up on what she'd been thinking, Chelsea turned to him in amazement. "What?"

"You seem to really enjoy this creative stuff. More than that," he continued, nodding to the neatly stacked set of printouts she'd moved aside to work on her sketches. "Maybe you should try doing more of it."

"My degree's in finance," she reminded him primly, "not marketing."

"So? Go back to school and get another one. Or set yourself up a sideline helping out small-business owners who're good with tools but not computers." Resting his arms on her desk, he added a wry grin. "Y'know, like me."

"Right," she parried with a laugh. "That's just what I need—more clients like you."

"Hey, I'm not so bad."

His wounded look was so convincing she couldn't resist ruffling his hair. "I suppose not. When you're not being impossible, you're almost bearable."

He chuckled. "I hate to tell you this, but that's the nicest thing a woman's said to me in a long time."

"I have no trouble believing that." She did her best to nail him with a haughty look, but it had no effect on him whatsoever, and she ended up smiling instead. "I really don't get to you, do I?"

His grin faded, mellowing into a pensive expression she'd seldom noticed on his face. "Only when you wear your hair down."

Flabbergasted didn't cover her reaction to that one. She searched his eyes for a sign that he was yanking her chain, but all she found was warm, honest admiration.

"I've been wondering something," he confided.

"Really? What's that?"

"If you'd like to go to the reunion with me. I mean, we're both going anyway, so it'd be fun. Unless you're going with someone else," he added hastily.

"Not yet." She let that hang in the air for a few seconds, then ended the suspense with a laugh. "Sure, I'll go with you. Thanks for asking."

"No problem." They were still grinning at each other when a familiar luxury sedan glided up to the millhouse and parked near the front porch. Boyd had been fast asleep under her desk, but the sound of the engine roused him, and he hopped up on the settee to stare out the window. His motion caught Daisy's attention and she leaped onto the sofa, scrambling up his back to the windowsill. Her fur spiked, and she arched her spine in an aggressive stance Chelsea had never seen before. Clearly spooked, she scrambled down and wedged herself under the stove, the white tip of her tail the only evidence that a cat had been there a moment ago.

"Yeah," Paul muttered. "That's how I feel around your dad, too."

"Well, get over it," Chelsea admonished him sternly. "I'm sure he's finishing up a call, but he probably won't be long. Put on your company manners."

She wished he had a clean shirt to put on, too, but there was nothing she could do about that now. Instead, she opened a drawer and swept the mess on her desk into it so her father wouldn't see what a slob she'd become. Closing the web program, she tried to pull up a spreadsheet that tracked the financials on the mill project but somehow managed to hit the shutdown icon instead.

"No, no, no," she muttered through clenched teeth, banging the button on her track pad as if that would help.

To her astonishment, Paul's hand closed over hers and pulled it away. When she glared up at him, he met her anger with calm reassurance. "That won't make it go any faster, you know."

"You don't understand," she all but whined.

"I understand your dad's here," he replied smoothly, resting her hand against his chest. "And you're shaking like a leaf."

For some insane reason, the sensation of his heart beating under her palm made her feel better. Blinking up at him, she saw compassion in his dark eyes, along with something else she couldn't quite identify. She'd seen them twinkle plenty of times, in amusement or mischief, depending on the situation. This was something entirely different, and instinct told her it was meant especially for her.

Fortunately, her laptop's start-up chime broke the strange mood that had taken over her office, and she backed away from him. Avoiding his gaze, she said, "I'm fine. Could you make sure the mill's ready for an inspection?"

"Are you serious? The guys bugged outta here like a tornado was coming, and it's a mess back there."

"I mean, set something up so Dad can see the saws working," she clarified while she opened the mercifully cooperative spreadsheet. "That's why he's here, after all."

Paul didn't respond, and she was afraid she'd offended him. When she glanced over, he shook his head with a wry grin. "You're really terrified of disappointing him, aren't you?"

"You can psychoanalyze me later," she snapped, pointing toward the business end of the mill. "For now, get that monster in gear so we can wow him. Please."

The last word was an afterthought, but apparently that was what he needed to get him moving. Giving her one of those knee-weakening grins, he ticked her nose with his finger. "Well, since you said 'please'…"

He sauntered out and closed the door behind him. Once they got through her father's visit, she vowed, she'd give Paul Barrett a very large—and very loud—piece of her mind. But right now she had bigger problems.

And they were walking through the front door.

Despite his expertly tailored suit and designer shoes, Theo Barnes was one tough customer. In fact, Paul mused while they continued their impromptu tour, this all-business banker would've given his former employer—a rugged lumber boss—a run for his money. He'd never thought about it before, but now it made sense that the man's eyes were green. Every other word out of his mouth was punctuated by dollar signs.

His obsession with numbers reminded Paul of Chelsea when they'd first started working together, and for the first time he recognized how far she'd come to meet him in the middle and make their current partnership a success. Her father was another story. Set in his ways, convinced he was right, he wasn't someone Paul could charm into trying another approach.

So he didn't even bother trying. Instead, when Theo

asked him a direct question, he answered it honestly. Otherwise, he kept his mouth shut. *Tense* wasn't the word for the normally casual atmosphere inside the millhouse. Even outgoing Boyd was hiding under the lobby bench, clearly hoping they'd forget about him.

Unfortunately, Paul didn't have that option, but he decided he'd done his best to defuse some of the tension that had accompanied their surprise visitor. He handed out ear protection and demonstrated how the restored waterwheel powered the saws. Once he'd shut everything down, he waited while they removed their headphones. He knew he'd done well with the resources at hand, and any other day, that would be enough for him. But he had to admit, he was more than a little anxious to hear what the man had to say.

When the whirring finally stopped, Theo swept Paul's domain with an assessing look. "It's remarkable how far you've gotten on such a small loan. With hiring a crew and purchasing such expensive raw material, how have you managed it?"

"Well, first off, Chelsea doesn't let me buy a bucket of nails without a purchase order and a good reason." Flashing her a grin, he was pleased to get a faint version of her usual smile in return. "Beyond that, the crew's volunteer, at least for now. When we get up and running, I'll be able to pay them for a few hours here and there. Except for my brother and me, the guys are retired, so they don't want to do too much anyway. Mostly, they enjoy being back here, just like I do."

"You're still convinced you'll be producing furniture by September?"

"Yes, sir," Paul answered, hoping he sounded more confident than he felt. The truth was, they *had* to be ready by then. Taking advantage of the holiday shopping season was his only chance to make this work in time for Granddad to see it. This time next year, it wouldn't matter anymore.

Theo cast a dubious look around the still-evolving work space, and Paul couldn't blame him. To an outsider, the mill area must appear to be nothing more than a collection of outdated machinery and spare parts. To him, it was already productive, if not exactly efficient.

Frowning, the banker shook his head. "You've made good progress, but you have a very small staff, and they're only here part-time. It's hard to believe you'll have anything to sell before the end of this year."

"Actually," Chelsea said, "Paul finished the first piece yesterday, completely manufactured on-site with legacy equipment. Would you like to see it?"

The description of his process was straight out of the promotional material she'd reviewed with him earlier, and Paul couldn't miss the hint of pride in her voice. Whatever the reason, he was pleased to see some of her spunk coming back. He didn't understand why, but the fact that she felt some ownership of the project made him happier than if it had been his alone.

While she held her father's gaze, disapproval showed on his face, and Paul got the feeling there was more going on here than he understood. One thing was obvious, even to him: she was struggling with something. Her voice was calm, but the tension in her jaw told him she was putting in a lot of effort to remain composed in front of her dad.

Hoping to ease some of the strain for her, Paul spoke up. "Why don't you and I take a look at it, sir? Chelsea's got numbers to crunch out front."

"They can wait," she retorted in a no-nonsense tone

only a fool would mess with. As if he hadn't gotten the message from that, her eyes snapped their own warning, and he wisely chose to go along.

"Fine by me." Motioning them toward the newly reclaimed back space, he explained, "Chelsea suggested we should make a real statement with our first piece. After ripping down some of our hundred-and-twenty-year-old oak, I made it into a dining table that'll seat fourteen people for the holidays."

When they stepped inside, he flipped the light switch and prayed Jason's newly installed can lights would all come on. They did, and he sent up a grateful look for the divine help. Because quite honestly, he hadn't tested them until just now. Apparently Chelsea knew that, because she gave him a subtle thumbs-up from the doorway. Quick as it was, the gesture made him feel as though he'd scored a winning goal for the team.

Their team, he realized with fresh appreciation for what they'd accomplished. Together, they'd nailed down financing, assembled a crew and worked like dogs to bring the abandoned mill to where it stood right now. They had only one table to show for it, but it was stunning. He'd kept it simple, using a matte finish to allow the natural beauty of the wood to shine through. Beneath the soft lighting, the hand-rubbed surface gleamed with a solid, ageless feel perfectly suited to its current surroundings.

"It's quite something," Theo acknowledged, walking around the table to view it from all angles. "How much do you think it will bring in?"

"I haven't gotten that far," Paul admitted. When he got a sharp look from the banker, he quickly went on. "You know a lot more about custom-made furniture than me. What do you think it's worth?"

Chelsea's slight nod told him he'd handled the question well, and he waited while Theo considered the unique table. When he finally named a figure, Paul came close to swallowing his tongue. Once he trusted himself to speak normally, he said, "That should work."

"I'd say so," Theo replied with an unexpected laugh. "Of course, that's the price for a CEO who's furnishing his lodge in Aspen and wants everything to be one of a kind. Around here, it wouldn't bring nearly that much."

"Huh." Father and daughter pinned him with curious stares, and he hunted for something more intelligent to say. "That makes sense, I guess."

"And of course, it's missing those fourteen chairs, isn't it?"

"Uh-huh." Suddenly, Paul seemed to be at a loss for words, and he gave himself a mental kick. Fortunately, his brain recovered and rapidly shifted gears into problem-solving mode. "I was thinking two armchairs, with two spindle-back benches on each side."

"Individual seating is better for most high-end buyers," Theo pointed out, launching into a series of suggestions for how they should be made.

Paul wasn't a detail person, and he sent Chelsea an SOS kind of look. Judging by her polite but closed-off expression, she had no intention of stepping into this conversation, and he was on his own. He did his best to absorb what Theo was telling him, nodding here and there to give the appearance of understanding. The truth was, as soon as this very intense man left, Paul was taking a long, quiet walk in the woods.

Now he understood why Chelsea had been so timid in

high school. Raised by a father who was quick to tell others what to do, she could either obey him or face a stern lecture about what she should've done differently. Even now, she wasn't exactly flexible, but she was a lot more willing to compromise than she'd been when they'd first started. Having experienced Theo's hammering treatment firsthand, Paul was even more impressed by her turnaround.

They were on their way back to the lobby when Theo casually said, "Chelsea, our board meeting is on Saturday at one, after we close for the day."

It wasn't an invitation, and a quick glance made it clear she didn't think much of his commanding tone. Theo expected her to attend that meeting, regardless of any other plans she might have made, and the man's high-handed attitude got Paul's hackles up.

Hoping to appear only mildly interested, he summoned a grin. "You're kidding, right? You have meetings on the weekend?"

"Yes, we do," Theo replied. "That way our administrative business doesn't interfere with our customers' needs."

What about your employees? Paul was dying to say, but he managed to keep his mouth shut. Coming from an outsider, the comment would only cause trouble. While he couldn't care less what this man thought of him personally, he was smart enough to recognize that being in Theo's good graces was crucial to keeping the flow of money coming from Shenandoah Bank.

While he struggled to rein in his own temper, he was astounded to hear Chelsea say, "I can't make it this time, Dad. I didn't hear about it until just now, and I have a commitment on Saturday."

Theo's shocked reaction made it clear he hadn't anticipated she would refuse, and Paul guessed it was the first time his daughter had ever disobeyed him. Unfortunately, his piercing eyes swung to Paul with a glare that could've blasted through solid steel. How he knew her plans included Paul was beyond him, but he carefully kept his expression neutral. He didn't want to appear to be gloating, but looking intimidated would be even worse.

After a long, uncomfortable staring contest, Theo shifted back to her. "I'm sure you can find a way to do both."

Without hesitation, she shook her head. "Our ten-year high school reunion is that night, and Paul invited me to go with him. I already said yes, and I'm not backing out now."

The tension Paul had noticed earlier was nothing compared to what crackled in the air now. It was so quiet he thought he could hear Boyd's stomach rumbling for lunch.

Finally, Theo's features creased with something that resembled acceptance and he offered his hand to Paul. "Thank you for taking time out of your schedule to give me a tour. Enjoy your weekend."

Sending his daughter a pained look, he went through the entryway and out to his car without breaking stride. Once the taillights were out of sight, Paul turned to Chelsea with a low whistle. "Whoa. I'm impressed."

"Yeah," she replied with a shaky laugh. "Me, too. I usually just go along with what he wants, so I've never done anything like that in my life. I'm not sure what came over me."

"Whatever it was, I'm glad you went with it," Paul assured her quickly. "You shouldn't let anyone push you around like that, not even your dad."

"I guess."

He could see she was regretting her tough stand, and he figured it might help to get all her fears out in the open so she could confront them and move ahead. "How do you think it'll play later on?"

"Not well. But since I've been here, I've realized it's time for me to live my own life, not the one he wants for me. By the time I get back to Roanoke he'll either have accepted that or not."

He'd done the same with his parents years ago, and he understood how much courage it took to blaze your own trail. Especially when the man you were rebelling against held your career in his manicured hands. "Sounds pretty brave to me. You've come a long way."

She hummed in reply, setting off his internal alarm. "What's wrong?"

"Maybe nothing, but I've got a bad feeling."

"Because of your dad?" Paul could relate to that. Theo Barnes had given him the chills ever since he was a kid.

Staring at his empty parking spot, she nodded. "He never gives up that easily, and it makes me wonder if he's up to something."

"With you or the mill?"

"I don't know," she confided with a frown. "But whatever it is, you can bank on it being good for him."

Paul chuckled to break the mood. "Bank on it. I get it."

That got him an irritated glare. "I wasn't trying to make a joke, Paul."

"I know," he answered smoothly. "That's what makes it funny."

"It's not—"

"Instead of fighting with me, why don't we eat while you show me the rest of the new website?"

She opened her mouth to protest, but he pretended

not to notice as he motioned for her to go into her office ahead of him. Rolling those gorgeous green eyes, she muttered something about men under her breath but followed his suggestion. As soon as Paul cracked open the fridge, their pets came running to claim their share of the subs he pulled out. Boyd was fairly polite about it, but the kitten stood on her hind legs, pawing his jeans with a pitiful meow.

"You scrounge," he chided the hopeful-looking hound. "You taught her to do that."

"Actually, that's my fault," Chelsea corrected him with a grin. "She loves people food, and it's nice to have company when I'm eating. I probably feed her too much of it, but she's so cute, I can't resist."

Flinging a piece of ham over to Boyd, he broke a corner off his Swiss cheese for Daisy and joined Chelsea at her desk. While they ate and chatted about promotion and other things he knew absolutely nothing about, Paul put Theo and his questionable motivations out of his mind. He wasn't about to spoil a pleasant lunch break with Chelsea worrying about things that were out of his control.

Chapter Eight

For the first time since graduating, Chelsea was in the Barrett's Mill High School gym, unpacking a box filled with mobiles strung with gold and silver stars. Since their senior-prom theme had been "Reach for the Stars," the committee had decided to carry it through to the reunion. Which meant the shiny decorations were perfect.

In theory, anyway. The reality was that the fishing line had a knack for knotting itself up, and every set she pulled free of the bubble wrap needed to be untangled. If she hadn't known better, she'd have thought her father arranged this exercise in frustration as punishment for defying his order to attend today's Shenandoah Bank board meeting.

She quickly banished the childish notion and got a folding chair from the rolling rack nearby. Sitting down, she picked up the first of twenty-four mobiles and got started.

"What a mess!" Brenda exclaimed from behind her. Crouching down, she rummaged through the packaging and groaned. "Oh, honey, this'll take you forever. Do you want some help?"

Out of long-standing habit, Chelsea almost refused the offer. Then again, even if their fearless chairman was the worst knot straightener in history, at least she was entertaining company. “Sure. Thanks.”

Brenda fetched another chair and plunked herself down opposite Chelsea. While she fiddled with a mobile, she said, “I heard your dad stopped by the mill.” Casting a glance up through her razor-cut bangs, she added, “Do you want to talk about it?”

“Why?”

Angling her head for a better look at the rat’s nest in her hands, she studiously avoided Chelsea’s gaze. “Well, I heard a few folks talking about it at Bible study last night. They saw him racing through town like he couldn’t leave fast enough. They were wondering if maybe you two had a dustup or something.”

“Were they?” Not long ago, she’d have considered their interest an intrusion into her very personal business. But now she understood that many of them were sincerely concerned about how she’d taken his impromptu visit. “It’s sweet of them to worry, but I’m fine.”

Brenda dropped her hands and pinned Chelsea with a you-don’t-fool-me look her kids probably dreaded. “If you don’t want to talk about it, fine. But don’t sit there and lie to me, Chelsea Lynn. I can tell you’re upset, even if you don’t want to admit it.”

The mild scolding caught her off guard, and she started spilling her guts. Quietly, of course. She didn’t need the entire decorating committee spreading around the fact that after a lifetime of blind obedience, she’d finally found the backbone to stand up to her domineering father.

When she stopped for air, Brenda’s eyes widened in

admiration. “Wow, that’s really something. Where did you find the guts to go up against him like that?”

Paul.

Unbidden, his name flashed into her mind, and Chelsea batted it away like an annoying gnat. But it came back again, flitting around just out of her reach. Since she’d returned to the faith she’d neglected for so long, that kind of thing had been happening more and more, forcing her to confront emotions she’d once have dismissed as utter foolishness.

Now that she thought about it, her confidence had been growing at more or less the same rate as her friendship with Paul. He listened to her, for one thing, taking her ideas seriously. Not that he was oblivious to her looks or anything. While he didn’t lay it on too thick, he often found clever ways to compliment her appearance. Her smile, the way her eyes sparked when she was mad at him. Which was frequently.

Since she wasn’t ready to confess her feelings to anyone just yet, she settled for a nice, safe response. “I’m not sure.”

“However you managed it, good for you. I’m an only child, just like you, and my parents didn’t give up that you’re-my-baby thing until I’d had one of my own. Now they dote on the kids and I can actually be myself.”

“If that’s what it takes,” Chelsea replied wryly, “I guess I’m sunk.”

That got her a coy look. “Don’t be too sure about that.”

“What on earth are you talking about?”

“Paul Barrett, of course. You work with him all day long. You must see how crazy he is about you.”

Laughing, Chelsea shook her head. “More like driving me crazy.”

"Whatever you say," she responded in a soothing tone she almost certainly used to end arguments with her husband. Her phone began singing "Girls Just Want to Have Fun," and she checked the caller ID. "It's Steve. Excuse me a minute."

"Take your time." Chelsea hung one of the rescued mobiles from the edge of a nearby table. "I'm not going anywhere."

Brenda laughed and headed into the hallway to have her conversation in relative privacy. It was still weird for Chelsea to think of her former classmates as wives and mothers. Most of her acquaintances in Roanoke were career-driven women with barely enough time to date, much less begin families. Here there were plenty of women her age who were settled. And happy. Not pining for something beyond their grasp, or clawing their way to the top of a mountain that seemed to get taller with each passing year.

On paper, she had everything she could possibly need, but watching the former pep-squad captain with her raucous, loving clan had confirmed her suspicion that there was more to life. She wanted what Brenda had, but she had no clue how to get it.

"Hey, there." Glancing over, she saw Paul walking toward her, a ladder balanced on his shoulder. More like strutting, actually, and she couldn't miss the feminine cooing drifting over from the table-setting crew. Apparently, he didn't notice the ruckus as he set down his load and assessed her situation with a quiet whistle. "What a disaster. Did they come like that?"

"Yes." Reaching down, she snatched another one from the box. "We ordered them that way."

His arrogant captain-of-the-team entrance had irked

her, and she didn't bother trying to hide it. Apparently, he wasn't good at reading body language, or he'd have back-pedaled the way most people did when she whipped out the sarcasm. That, or he didn't care. Instead, he laughed and helped himself to Brenda's chair. Even when she arched an eyebrow and leveled a cool stare at him, he just grinned. Finally, when she'd run out of ammunition, she gave in to a smile.

"There it is," he congratulated her, ticking the tip of her nose with his finger. "I knew it was in there somewhere."

That he'd kept at it until she relented made her want to do more than smile, but she cautioned herself about getting carried away with this guy. She wouldn't be in Barrett's Mill a day longer than necessary, and starting anything more serious than what they had now would only end in hurt feelings. "What are you doing here, anyway?"

"You have mobiles." He indicated the decorations dangling from the table "I have a really tall ladder."

"We need hooks." In reply, he held up the hardware bag he was carrying. Unlike most men, he always seemed to be one step ahead of her, but there was no way she'd tell him that. His ego barely fit in the door as it was. "Don't think I'm impressed or anything."

"Never."

Flashing her another grin, he looped a few of the mobiles over one hand, picked up his ladder with the other and headed for the other end of the gym. Along the way, he greeted everyone by name, stopping so often to chat that it took him nearly five minutes to cross the floor.

Not that she was keeping track, of course. Her task wasn't the most challenging, and his glad-handing was a welcome distraction. She wished she had his way with people, she thought wistfully. He had a God-given talent for making others feel at ease, something she'd experienced herself many times.

It had been Paul who'd made the first tentative steps in their friendship, encouraging her to meet him in the middle. Their forced partnership might easily have been sheer torture, something she endured because it was her job. Instead, she'd found herself enjoying this assignment more than any in her career. Paul had a lot to do with that. His easygoing personality and tolerant style were a good balance for her more intense approach to—well, everything.

Somehow, along the way they'd left their rivalry behind and become friends. They'd learned to have faith in each other, to trust that they were coming from different angles but would eventually wind up in the same place. She couldn't have imagined it that first stressful day, but sitting there watching him, hearing his voice echo through the wide-open space, she felt her mouth lift into a little smile.

In spite of her best attempts to remain detached and professional, Paul had come to mean a lot to her. She was really going to miss him when she left.

On his way to pick up Chelsea, Paul took a detour and stopped at the florist. Since this was technically a high school dance, he figured it'd be nice if he brought Chelsea some kind of corsage to wear.

When he explained what he needed, the twentysomething clerk immediately asked, "What color is her dress?"

Paul opened his mouth to answer, then realized he had no clue what outfit she'd chosen for tonight. With a helpless male gesture, he replied, "I'm not sure, so let's keep it simple."

"This is really pretty." Pulling out a cluster of tiny white and yellow roses, she added a dimpled smile. "Your girlfriend will like it."

"Could you tuck some of those miniature daisies in there? I'll pay extra."

"Okay."

He could tell from her reaction that people didn't normally add wildflowers to a classy wrist bouquet. He nearly told her to forget about it, then stopped. Chelsea liked daisies, and appropriate or not, he knew she'd appreciate the personal touch.

The clerk put his purchase in a clear box and tied it up with a pink ribbon before swiping his credit card. On his way out the door, she called, "Have fun!"

He waved a thank-you and finished his trip to Chelsea's place. After parking in the Donaldsons' driveway, he noticed them sitting on the front porch and went up to say hello.

"Don't you look handsome?" Lila cooed, looking him over from head to toes. "All those girls'll be fighting over who gets to dance with you tonight."

"Just like old times." He chuckled. Daisy was sacked out in Hank's lap, and he reached down to rub her forehead. Meeting Hank's gaze, he added, "Speaking of which, the new saw you installed works like a charm. How'd you guys manage to integrate it with that old rigging?"

"A trick here and there. Nothing a youngster would understand."

Translation: *if I tell you, you won't need me anymore.* Recognizing the purpose behind that cryptic response, Paul replied, "Then I guess we're gonna have to keep you guys around awhile. Maybe work out some kinda pay scale. How would that suit you?"

"We'll talk," Hank grumbled, but the interested gleam in his eyes told Paul he'd hit the right button with the old foreman.

"Anytime. Right now, though, Chelsea and I are taking a trip down memory lane."

As he headed back down the steps, he heard Hank chortling while his wife whispered for him to behave himself. He'd been getting that kind of reaction from people a lot lately, Paul mused while he strolled down the path to the old carriage house. It seemed that whenever he mentioned Chelsea, folks assumed it meant something.

Then again, he did say her name quite a bit these days. When they were working together it was inevitable, but he suddenly realized they spent a lot of their free time together, too. Going over the week's progress over lunch at The Whistlestop on Saturdays, sitting with his family at church on Sundays. He even bumped into her at the grocery store on occasion. Of course, in a tiny place like Barrett's Mill, it was tough to avoid anyone, even if you wanted to.

And he definitely wasn't trying to avoid Chelsea. In fact, he enjoyed spending time with her. If he was completely honest, he'd have to admit—at least to himself—that he'd actually been trying to see more of his beautiful business partner, not less.

Looking down at the corsage box in his hands, he groaned at his own foolishness. A smart, elegant lady like her wasn't interested in starting up anything with a guy like him. With a hound, a 1930s truck and a mountain of debt to his name, he had less than nothing to offer her. Even if she might personally like him, his aimless lifestyle had turned off every woman he'd ever known. There was no reason for her to be any different.

Resigned to the notion that this evening was just about two friends going to a dance with some other friends, Paul knocked on the paned window in the door and waited for her to answer. It was a studio apartment, so he could see everything from where he stood. When she appeared from around the corner, he casually waved like someone who hadn't just been standing on her front stoop, arguing with himself.

She was wearing an emerald-green dress that rippled like water when she moved. By the time she opened the door, those errant feelings he'd shoved away returned with a vengeance. The temptation to wrap her in his arms and kiss her was so strong he rooted his feet in place to keep from acting on it.

Her confused look was a perfect complement to the two mismatched earrings she had on. "Were we supposed to meet here?"

"Nah," he said, hoping he sounded cool. "Just thought you might like a ride up to the school."

"I would, thanks. Come on in."

She stepped aside to let him in, but he carefully stayed near the door, far away from the scent of gardenias that seemed to follow her everywhere. She always looked polished and put-together, but tonight there was an extra sparkle to her. It was enough to make his brain struggle for something to say. Then out popped "Did you know you've got two different earrings on?"

He bit back a groan at the stupid comment, but thankfully she laughed. "I can't decide which style looks better with this dress."

Personally, Paul thought the outfit needed absolutely

nothing but the woman inside it, but he seized on the opportunity to cover his blunder. Angling his head for a closer look, he pointed to the left one. "All those dangly crystals will catch the light better."

"Dangly crystals it is." She plucked out the other one and replaced it with the chandelier type that matched the one he'd chosen.

Remembering the flowers, he thrust the box toward her. "This is for you."

She took out the corsage and inhaled. "They smell wonderful, and I love the daisies."

"They're your favorite," he said, as if she didn't know that.

"That was very sweet of you," she added, beaming up at him with the most incredible smile he'd ever seen in his life.

He'd resolved to keep his distance, but he felt himself moving toward her. Drawn in by those dazzling green eyes, the affection lighting her face. Helpless to resist the pull of her, he settled his hands lightly at her waist, giving her room to pull away. She didn't.

Grinning down at her, he said, "I can be sweet."

"Really?" she challenged him, her cute nose tilted in the air. "I hadn't noticed."

The urge to lean in and kiss her was almost overwhelming, but he was hesitant to spoil the moment. Instead, he chuckled. "I let you pick the music for our dance tonight, didn't I? Didn't even ask what it was. I think that should count for something."

"I suppose so," she agreed with a coy smile. "I mean, for all you know, it's a Viennese waltz."

He didn't doubt for a second that she knew the steps to all the waltzes, Viennese or otherwise. That she was teasing him this way sent a warm current through every nerve, and he was thrilled that they'd finally gotten past all the roadblocks to meet at this point. She trusted him, he realized with a jolt. Trusted him to hold her this way and not take advantage, to understand her wry humor and respond in kind.

He'd always believed God created a match for everyone, and that if he kept looking, someday he'd find the woman meant for him. Could Chelsea be the one? he wondered. It was quite possibly the nuttiest idea he'd ever had, and the longer it caromed around in his head, the crazier it seemed.

Then again, he'd always gone the safe route, sticking with someone until it became obvious to him that it was time to move on. That time had come and gone in his relationship with Chelsea, and he was still here. It must mean something, but he wasn't ready to think about it just now.

"Ready to go?" When she nodded, he opened the door for her and followed her out to his truck. When they were settled inside, he asked, "Are you gonna tell me which song you picked for our dance?"

That got him a lofty smirk. "Why don't you guess?"

"Was it a song from our senior prom?"

"I wouldn't know."

Astonished by the revelation, he twisted in his seat to stare at her. "You didn't go?"

"Nobody asked me."

"You could've gone on your own," he reasoned as he pulled onto the street. "I did."

She laughed. "So you could dance with all the girls you wanted, no doubt. Is that your plan for tonight, too?"

A couple of weeks ago, it would've been. But something had changed, and while he didn't completely understand it, he decided to follow his instincts and see where they took him. "Nope. I'm all yours."

She lifted one skeptical eyebrow. "Am I supposed to get all gooey now?"

Gooey wasn't really her style, but he decided to play along just for fun. "Only if you want to."

"I think I'll pass. Thanks anyway."

With that, she turned to look out the open window. Dressed for an upscale evening and framed by the colors of a summer sunset, she just about took his breath away. The tires sank into the loose gravel beyond the pavement, and Paul firmly steered his attention back to the road before he ran them into a tree or something.

"Oh, look at you two!" Brenda exclaimed when they arrived, snapping a picture before they were even in the door. "You look fabulous together. Don't they, Steve?"

"Definitely." Obviously humoring his wife, the patient man gave Paul a hang-in-there glance before trailing after Brenda on her way to the stage.

"I don't know how he does it," Paul murmured while he grabbed two cups of punch from the drinks table. "She'd wear me out in a week."

Sipping her drink, Chelsea shrugged. "I guess when someone's really important to you, you learn to love all the parts of them."

"You ever get that far with anyone?" He hadn't meant to say it out loud, but now that he had, he did his best to come across as curious instead of as though he was dying to hear her response.

"Not really," she confided with a wry smile. "A few times I thought I had, but they turned out to be more fondness than love. How 'bout you?"

"Me neither. I mean, I like women, but they all kinda blend together after a while."

Except for you, he added silently. Now that he'd acknowledged his growing feelings for Chelsea, the thought of her leaving in a couple of weeks started gnawing at his gut. When had he decided she was special? Searching his memory, he couldn't come up with anything. But that didn't change the fact that somewhere along the line he'd stopped viewing her as a business associate and started seeing her as something more. The big question was, now that he did, what was he going to do about it?

The answer to that surfaced when the DJ's quick-tempo song ended and he announced, "Okay, now we're going to slow things down a little. I hear your valedictorian and salutatorian are here somewhere. Paul Barrett and Chelsea Barnes, come on up."

Taking Chelsea's cup, Paul set them both down and crooked his arm, gentleman-style. After a moment she took it, and they strolled toward the area right in front of the stage. Amid the cheers and catcalls, she turned pleading eyes on him and whispered, "I know your buddies are watching, but please don't embarrass me."

Taking her hands in his, he met that hesitant look with an encouraging smile. "Never."

After a deep breath, she nodded to the DJ, who cued up the song she'd chosen. Paul recognized it as something he'd heard on her playlist just the other day. A sweet country ballad about old friends who run into each other unexpectedly and end up falling in love under the stars.

He wasn't prone to romantic visions, but with Chelsea in his arms and all those sparkling mobiles spinning overhead, the song couldn't have been more perfect. As more couples joined them, he asked, "Is this supposed to be about us?"

He'd expected her to laugh, or maybe zing him with the kind of sharp comeback he'd gotten accustomed to hearing from this very spirited woman. Instead, her lips curved invitingly. "You tell me."

Before he knew what was happening, Paul felt himself leaning in to kiss her. At the last moment, he regained some of his senses and diverted to brush his lips across her cheek. She bathed him in a warm, grateful smile, which he took as his reward for honoring his promise not to embarrass her.

As the song continued, she relaxed into his arms, and it took everything he had not to pull her close for a real kiss. They'd spent so much time together over the summer, this very personal connection to her felt natural and bizarre at the same time. He'd never regarded Chelsea that way, but apparently his emotions had taken a different turn when his brain wasn't paying attention.

This evening wasn't going quite the way he'd anticipated. The trouble was, he couldn't determine if that was good or bad.

What a night!

Giving in to the warm, fuzzy sensation of being wrapped in those strong arms, Chelsea rested her cheek on Paul's chest as their first song led into another soft ballad. She'd taken a real chance, choosing such sentimental music for a dance that spotlighted them in front of so many people. He could've easily held her at a proper distance, chatting with her until the music stopped and they could go their separate ways.

But he hadn't.

She could still picture the shards of light reflected in his dark eyes, adding to the twinkle she often saw there when he looked at her. Those glances had become more frequent lately, and while they'd reviewed her website changes, she'd been treated to quite a few of them. More than the usual male interest she was used to seeing, they'd shone with admiration for the effort she was putting in to make his family's business viable again.

Paul appreciated her in a way she hadn't experienced before. That appreciation had prompted her to take the biggest leap of her life and let him know she considered him more than a friend. Discovering he shared her feelings thrilled—and terrified—her.

Their new status was a fragile thing, she realized, and she wasn't at all certain about what came next. But she knew enough not to fill the cozy space between them with questions neither of them was ready to face. For now, she was grateful just to be here with him. Whatever happened, she knew this single perfect moment would stay in her memory forever.

Thankfully, the DJ switched over to a retro line dance, calling for everyone to join in while he coached them through the steps. The quicker tempo and clumsy dancing soon had everyone laughing while they sang along and tried not to injure each other. When things started getting out of hand, Steve and Paul guided Brenda and Chelsea in between them.

"There," Paul said in between laughs. "Now you're safe."

While the crowd spun around for the next pattern, Brenda caught Chelsea's arm and leaned close. "What on earth did you do to Paul? I've never seen him like this."

Flattered that someone else had noticed his behavior, she decided it was best to play dumb. "Like what?"

"So focused on one girl. I mean, he used to flirt with everyone in the place, but tonight it's like you're the only one here."

That was exactly how she felt, and Chelsea's heart soared with delight. "We're just having fun, like everyone else."

"Right," she drawled with a long, suspicious look. "Well, you make sure to invite me to the wedding. Don't forget that dance was my idea."

As the group peeled off into two separate halves, Chelsea briefly wondered if Brenda seriously thought she and Paul might get married someday. For all Brenda's flightiness, while working on the reunion she'd learned that her old classmate had keen instincts when it came to people. If she'd noticed some deeper connection between Chelsea and Paul, it was probably for real.

If it was, how would she handle something like that? Her feelings for him were a confusing jumble of past resentment and present fondness, which made it tough for her to sort through whatever was going on between them now. While she'd all but arranged the circumstances so she could more accurately assess their puzzling relationship, she wasn't sure what to make of the result.

Obviously, Paul felt something more for her than friendship, but what? And just as important, what did she feel for him? It didn't take much for her to envision them as a couple, but as strong-willed as they both were, she couldn't deny they'd have a challenging road ahead of them. Different in so many ways, they shared some fundamental qualities that made compromising difficult. Working with him at the mill had made that abundantly clear to her, yet here she was, contemplating getting involved with a man who aggravated her on a nearly hourly basis. But then he'd grin, and she'd laugh, and they'd agree to disagree.

Could that work in a relationship? she wondered. And if it didn't, what then? She'd come to rely on Paul's steady optimism to brighten her days and provide some balance for her more serious nature. If a romance with him ended badly, she'd lose all that and be on her own again.

The music changed, and she put the dilemma out of her mind to concentrate on the new steps. For all intents and purposes, she was getting a do-over of the senior prom she'd missed the first time around, and she was determined to enjoy every minute of it.

It was long past midnight when Paul pulled into the Donaldsons' driveway. A single light was on in an upstairs window, and he couldn't help grinning. No doubt Hank would have something to say to him at church about keeping Chelsea out so late. Fortunately, the evening he'd spent with her was totally worth the scolding.

Putting an arm around her shoulders, he walked her down the moonlit path to the carriage house. When they reached her front door, the automatic light popped on to show her smiling up at him.

"Thanks for everything, Paul. I had a great time."

"Me, too."

Taking her hands, he gradually reeled her in, giving her time to move away. Her smile deepened, and he held her close as he dropped in for a kiss. Still leery of rushing things with her, he broke away, only to have her pull him in for another, much longer one. Standing in the moonlight with Chelsea, Paul was more content than he'd ever been in his life. Step by hesitant step, she'd drawn him in until there was nowhere for him to go but into her arms.

Toying with her earring, he asked, "You have any idea how long I've wanted to do that?"

"Why didn't you say so?"

"I didn't want you to think I was one of those guys," he confided. "How'd I do?"

"Very well, actually. I was beginning to think there was something wrong with me."

Picking up on her lighter tone, he gave her a quick once-over. "Not that I've noticed."

That got him a bright laugh, and much as he'd love to stay longer, he worried about the consequences to her reputation. Not to mention his own hide. "I really hate to go, but if I don't, Hank'll be out here with his shotgun."

"Probably," she agreed with a laugh.

With a parting kiss, she unlocked her door and went inside. Once he heard the dead bolt turn, he plunged his hands in his pockets and trudged back up the walkway. As he was driving away, he glanced into the rearview mirror and saw the Donaldsons' upstairs window go dark. Chuckling to himself, he leaned over to adjust the radio and noticed Chelsea's wrap on the seat.

Picking it up, he caught the scent of her perfume and instantly flashed back to their first dance earlier that night. When his memories led him to their tender kiss in the moonlight, he gave in to his emotions with a sigh. Now that he associated the scent of gardenias with the most amazing woman he'd ever met, he knew he'd never think of them the same way again.

The Barretts never did anything in a small way.

Chelsea was struck by that thought more than once

while she helped prepare a Sunday lunch that rivaled the size of most brunches she'd enjoyed. Once she'd rolled out of bed, of course. Now that her life ticked along on a more relaxed schedule, she'd left her night-owl habits behind for a more early-to-bed-early-to-rise kind of lifestyle. And, to her amazement, she actually preferred it.

Since Will wasn't strong enough to attend services, Pastor Griggs had stopped in to deliver his sermon again in private for Will and Olivia.

Hearing the muted voices in the dining room, Chelsea smiled at Diane while she picked up another tomato to slice for the salad. "It's so nice of him to come by just for them. How long has he been doing that?"

"Since Dad got home from the hospital. Before that, he met them at Cambridge Memorial to make sure they didn't feel cut off from the church."

More impressed than ever, Chelsea paused midchop. "That's incredible."

"That's Barrett's Mill," Diane commented. "It might be small, but when there's trouble around here, everyone pitches in to help."

The nostalgic tone of her voice reflected how Chelsea had been feeling lately. "It sounds like you miss it."

"I do, but when he had to close the mill, Tom was miserable here. It was too hard for him to keep seeing the people who lost their jobs, not because of anything they did wrong, but because the economy drove their company out of business."

"Some of the old crew is back at work," Chelsea pointed out. "They don't blame Will or Tom for losing their jobs."

"God bless them for that. Tom still couldn't stand to walk down the street and think there might have been something he could've done to keep the mill going. So when my parents retired to Florida and we had a chance to buy their house, we did. It's only a few miles away, but the distance and new position at the power plant made things much better for him."

"And for you?" Chelsea blurted without thinking. When Diane gave her a direct look, she realized she couldn't backpedal but tried to soften the impertinent question. "I mean, you raised your family here. It must've been hard to leave all that behind."

Understanding lit the older woman's eyes, and she gave Chelsea an encouraging smile that reminded her of Paul's. "Sometimes, but I reconnected with old friends in Cambridge, and my teen program at the church makes a real difference for kids who'd go home to an empty house otherwise. My life has taken a few odd turns, but I ended up where God meant for me to be. I can't think of anything better than that."

Diane patted her shoulder and picked up the large salad bowl to take it out to one of the picnic tables. There was a stack of pots and pans soaking in the farmhouse sink, and Chelsea decided to take care of them so the Barrett women could enjoy their guests. Tying on a bibbed apron that read Kiss the Cook, she picked up a scrubber and got to work.

The mindless job gave her time to mull over what Diane had said. It wasn't a secret that Chelsea and Paul had been getting closer throughout the summer, so it was no surprise his mother had picked up on Chelsea's dilemma: Stay in Barrett's Mill and see what happened, or return to the life she'd so carefully plotted and continue toward her goal of taking over the reins at Shenandoah Bank when her father retired? The first path led to something she'd only recently begun to consider, while the second took her toward the finish line of a race she'd been running for ten years.

Outside the window, she caught a glimpse of Paul with his two-year-old nephew on his shoulders, chatting with a neighbor. The pose seemed so natural to him, even while he took crackers from a small container and handed them up to his passenger. The toddler wasn't the neatest eater, and she wondered if Paul knew his vintage Hank Aaron jersey was covered in orange specks.

Then again, she thought as she resumed her scrubbing, even if he did, he probably wouldn't care. For Paul, family was everything, and a little mess was no big deal. From snack crumbs to the huge responsibility of reviving the old mill, he took on whatever needed doing with a cheerfulness that astounded her. The arrogant jock who'd strutted through their high school years had become a kind, caring man any woman would be proud to call her own.

Even you, a tiny voice whispered in the back of her mind.

This wasn't the first time she'd heard it, but now she chose to listen. Because somehow, when she wasn't looking, she'd drifted into love with Paul. Not the reckless kind of passion her parents' failed marriage had been made of, but a strong, steady kind of emotion that could sustain two people during a lifetime together.

That was her true dream, but in order to get it, she'd have to surrender the high-powered career she'd worked so hard for. As someone accustomed to cautiously analyzing her options, taking that leap of faith was more than scary. It was petrifying.

While she stood there, caught in the middle of a battle between her heart and her head, Paul happened to glance up at the kitchen window. When he saw her there, he gave her the same warm, affectionate smile that had caught her off guard last night. Seeing it now, in a less intimate setting, confirmed what she'd been mulling over since their nostalgic dance.

The question was, what should she do about it?

Fortunately, her cell phone began buzzing in her pocket, saving her from further soul-searching. She hadn't done much of it in her life, and even though she knew God was directing her steps, examining her emotions still wasn't all that comfortable for her.

When she saw her father's name on the screen, she let out a groan. On a Sunday? Did he never take a day off? Summoning patience, she tapped the answer icon. "Hi, Dad. How are you today?"

"Busy," he replied gruffly. "I need you back at the bank this week, sooner rather than later."

That seemed ominous, but she did her best to sound calm. "Is something wrong?"

"No." Apparently he realized he'd come across too strong and adjusted his tone to something less doom and gloom. "But circumstances have changed, and I'm recalling you."

"What?" she blurted, then caught herself and framed her protest in a more adult way. "It doesn't make sense to do that now, with the project so close to being finished. The grand reopening is in two weeks, and I'll be leaving after that."

"Paul's a clever young man. I'm sure he can manage a few picnic details without you."

Delivered with the weight of a royal proclamation, his statement was so condescending she bristled with anger. Paul's advice about not letting anyone push her around echoed in her memory, and she stiffened her spine for some long overdue rebellion. "I've put a lot of effort into this restoration, and there's no way I'm leaving so many things unfinished for someone else to do. I'll be back in Roanoke when I promised."

She nearly added, "And then I'm all yours," but she clamped her mouth shut before she could promise something she wasn't 100 percent committed to. Working with Paul had given her a chance to try new things and develop some creative skills she'd never realized she had. He trusted her judgment, and she enjoyed the different challenges she met from one day to the next.

While her banking position was stable and predictable, devoting so much of her time and energy to it might not suit her anymore. Maybe it was time for a change, maybe not. But that was up to her, not her father. The dutiful daughter in her recoiled from the very idea of defying him, but in her heart she was afraid if she didn't do it now, she might not get another chance.

"I see," he said quietly. "That's your final word?"

"Yes." Even to her own ears, that sounded harsh, so she softened her stance a bit. "In the meantime, if you need anything, I'd be happy to consult over the phone."

She hadn't even finished speaking when the line went silent. After saying his name a couple of times, she figured he'd hung up and shut off her phone. That feeling of dread slithered back in, and she was scowling when Paul appeared in the doorway.

"Whoa, that's not a good look," he said as he joined her near the sink. "Something wrong?"

There was no point in both of them worrying about her father's strange behavior, so she kept it to herself. "Dad wanted me to come back to the bank now, and I told him no."

"You're kidding."

"I wish."

"Well, good for you." When she grimaced, though, he frowned. "Whattya think he'll do?"

"I'm not sure," she confessed with a sigh. "But he's fired people for insubordination before, so I suppose it's a possibility."

"Not his own daughter." When she nodded, he brushed her fears away with a reassuring grin. "Well, there's a spot for you at the mill. If you want it, it's yours."

Her hero, she thought wistfully. Always there when she needed him, ready with a solution. Because Paul was the kind of guy who took care of the people around him, rather than expecting things to be the other way around. "I love working there, so I just might take you up on that. What are you doing in here, anyway?"

Taking the scrub brush from her, he announced, "It's time to quit doing dishes and come have some fun with us."

He'd noticed her working and wanted her to enjoy herself instead. His thoughtful gesture touched her in a way she was still getting used to. "I wanted to help your mom."

"I'm sure she appreciates that, but she'd probably remind you that even God rested once in a while."

"That sounds like her." She reached behind her to undo the apron string, but it had worked itself into a knot, and she turned around. "I can't reach it. Could you help me out?"

"Sure."

After a few seconds, she felt the ties fall away and spun to face him again. Affection warmed his gaze, and he slipped his arms around her the way he had last night.

Not tight, but not loose, either. It was more of a hold than a hug, as if he was testing to see how close she'd allow him to get.

Neither of them spoke, but the admiration glowing in his dark eyes reached every part of her, warming her straight down to her bare toes. Glancing around to make sure they were more or less alone, he gathered her into his arms for a kiss so intense it actually made her head spin. Even after he broke the kiss, he kept her close, which was fine with her. She wasn't in a hurry for him to let go.

Flashing a wry grin, he shook his head. "Y'know, I still can't believe it took me so long to figure out how amazing you are."

Because it was such a sweet, wonderful thing for him to say, she decided the time had come for her to take a more gracious view of their less-than-stellar past.

"Well, you know what they say. Better late than never."

Chapter Nine

Monday afternoon, Paul stopped by the office to drop off one of the purchase orders Chelsea insisted he use whenever they needed supplies. This one was for various-sized drill bits, and while he still didn't see the point of doing them, he'd filled it out the way she'd taught him, just to be nice. Since he'd started making more of an effort to follow the rules she set up, he'd sensed a shift in her attitude toward him. Less combative, more cooperative.

A green van pulled up near the porch, and he chuckled when he saw the floral motif painted on the side. "Did you order plants or something?"

"No." Leaning back in her chair, she peered out the front window. "Maybe he's lost."

When the deliveryman came inside, Paul could barely see him past the armload of red roses he was carrying. From behind them came a muffled "Delivery for Chelsea Barnes."

"What on earth? Just put them on that table behind you," she added in her usual pragmatic way. "They must weigh a ton."

"Pretty near." Once he was free of the two huge crystal vases, he held out a digital reader for her to sign and waved off her tip. "That's been taken care of, Ms. Barnes. Have a good day."

Once he was gone, Chelsea went over to the flowers. Curious but trying not to show it, Paul watched her slide the embossed florist card from its envelope. Her sour expression told him she wasn't pleased with some poor sap's extravagant gesture, and for some reason that made him smile. "Wrong number?"

"Definitely." Waving the card at him, she added, "They're from Alex."

Pushing off from the wall, he strolled over to join her.

Over her shoulder, he read, "'Pretty flowers for a pretty lady—Alex.'" Apparently, the Harvard boy didn't know daisies were her favorite, Paul mused with a grin. Point for the country boy. "Somebody's nervous."

"What do you mean by that?"

"When you skipped a business meeting to go to the reunion, your dad must've figured there's something going on between us. So when he got back, he told Alex that if he wants to stake his claim, he better do it quick."

"That's absurd," she protested.

"I know that, and you know that, but in case you haven't noticed, folks have a funny way of assuming things about us."

"That's true, I guess." Flipping the edge of the card, she frowned down at it.

Before he could ask what was wrong, his mother's well-traveled SUV pulled up outside. When she and Gram got out and headed for the porch, he hurried to open the door for them.

"Good morning, ladies. What're you doin' all the way out here?"

"Chelsea asked me to make some new curtains and seat cushions for the lobby," Gram explained. "Diane and I are here to measure so we can buy the fabric and start sewing today. Oh, what beautiful roses!" she cooed, burying her nose in the nearest bouquet. "They smell wonderful, don't they?"

"Why don't you each take a vase of them with you?" Chelsea suggested. "If they stay here, one of the pets will knock them over, or they'll get covered in sawdust."

"Are you sure?" Gram asked, obviously hesitant to take advantage of her generosity.

"I insist. I really can't keep them, and you'll be doing me a favor."

"All right, then, but only if you agree to come with us."

Chelsea laughed. "I don't know the first thing about sewing. That's why I called in the experts."

"We insist," Mom prodded with that no-nonsense look of hers. "I'm sure Paul can spare you for a few hours."

Actually, he wasn't crazy about the idea of the three of them strolling around trading stories about him, but since they'd agreed to take the irritating flowers away, he figured it was a good trade. "Sure, no problem. Do you need me to go hang out with Granddad?"

"Your father's got that covered," his mother replied with a laugh. "When we left, Will was setting up the chessboard, so they should be well occupied while we're gone."

"Poor Dad." Shaking his head in sympathy, he noticed that Gram looked perkier than she had in a long time. She was always cheerful, but her demeanor often had a determined quality to it, as if she was trying hard to keep everyone's spirits up. This morning she appeared lighter, as if she was grateful to escape her worries for a little while.

Suddenly, what she'd said registered more fully, and he slanted a peeved look at Chelsea. "You asked her?"

She opened her mouth to reply, but Gram interrupted. "Paul, we need to measure the windows. Could you move the furniture away from them, please?"

"Sure."

Shoving the bench and chairs aside, he left her and Mom to fuss over the measuring tape and discuss fabric colors. Then he motioned for Chelsea to follow him out to the side yard. She didn't hang back at all, and once they were out of earshot, she cut off his simmering temper with a hand in the air.

"Before you start in on me, do you remember the day when your mom was signaling me at church?" He gave a curt nod, and she continued. "When I called later, she said Olivia wanted to help with the restoration but needed a job she could do at home. I told her I'd come up with something and let her know. This is it."

"Don't you think she's got enough to do, taking care of Granddad all day long?"

"I do," she replied gently. "But your mom felt it was important for her to be part of the mill project. They've both been so good to me, I didn't have the heart to refuse them."

Her sentimental reasoning tugged at his own emotions, but he still had a point to make. "I just wish you'd asked me first."

"It had nothing to do with you."

That riled his settling temper, and he started winding up for another pitch. Then she smiled at him. Not the goading kind she nailed him with when she one-upped him, but the soft, adoring one that kept appearing in his dreams. "What?"

"I just think it's sweet how you worry about people, that's all."

Planting a kiss on his cheek, she went back to their guests with the kind of swagger he normally only associated with men. She'd come a long way in the past few weeks, he thought in admiration, and he was proud of her. She hadn't taken him up on his offer of a job, but she hadn't given him a definitive no, either. The idea of her staying on at the mill appealed to him more than it should have, and he had to admit it wasn't only her business sense he'd come to value.

In other words, he was dangerously close to the point of no return he'd always been so careful to avoid. Hover short of it, and you were fine. Go one step too far, and you were doomed.

The day before the grand reopening, Paul got an earlier start than usual. When he stepped out of his truck at the mill, he was greeted by the crisp scent of freshly sawed wood, laced with something nutty drifting on the early-morning breeze. Chelsea was curled up in one of the Adirondack chairs he'd made for the front porch, a steaming mug cradled in her hands. As he got closer, he saw it was dark blue, with Jenna's rendering of the mill and rushing stream painted in a mellow bronze color. Barrett's Sawmill and Barrett's Mill, Virginia, were spelled out beneath.

Classy and to the point, he thought. Just like the woman who'd helped design them. Another mug sat on the low table, and he grinned when he realized that she'd not only been told he was on his way, but had his favorite blend of gourmet caffeine waiting for him. Seeing his grandmother's influence here, he shook his head and decided to just go with it.

"Morning," he greeted her as he sprawled out in the other chair.

When she swiveled her head to smile over at him, he felt his heart roll over in his chest. If he needed any proof that his growing feelings for her were real, this was it. He'd never done emotional somersaults for any other woman, and while it should have made him happy, it actually did the opposite. His life was unsettled now, to say the least, and if the mill tanked again, he had no idea where he'd be this time next year. It wouldn't be fair to start something with Chelsea when he wasn't sure he could finish it.

"Correct me if I'm wrong," he began in a light tone, "but shouldn't you be scrambling around fixing last-minute glitches for the picnic?"

"I would, if there were any," she assured him with a cute little smirk. "Jenna will be here at ten to install your new signage, and I just confirmed the picnic layout with Molly. Bruce is on his way over to set up his barbecue equipment and the grills for hot dogs and hamburgers. Tomorrow's forecast is seventy-five and sunny, and you've got a hundred RSVPs, so I've allowed for twenty-five surprises."

Being a wing-it kind of guy himself, Paul continually marveled at her ability to not only plot out things in such detail but also allow for contingencies that would never occur to him. Sipping his coffee, he said, "Sounds like you've thought of everything, as usual."

In response, she held out what looked suspiciously

like a check. When he saw the amount, he came close to doing a comedic spit take. "What's this?"

"Dad's comments about finding a buyer for the oak dining set got me thinking. One of my sorority sisters just bought a lodge in the Catskills up in New York, and she's been hunting for furniture that's classic but has a rustic feel to it."

"I guess that dining set fits the bill."

"Definitely. When I called her, she said she needs something that can seat their extended family when they come over the summer and for holidays," Chelsea continued with a proud smile. "I emailed her those high-res photos we took for the website, and she went bonkers over it. She didn't want to risk losing out, so she overnighted the whole purchase price."

Still a little stunned, he glanced at the check again, hardly daring to believe all those zeros were real. "This is fantastic. I never could've made it happen without you."

When he met her gaze, interest sparked in her eyes, and she shifted to face him. "Really?"

It dawned on him that she could easily misinterpret his praise as something more personal, and he attempted to dial things back into a safer zone. "Really. Like I said before, if you're ever looking for a job, let me know."

Her expression dimmed considerably, and she relaxed back into her chair. Apparently, he wasn't the only one feeling things he shouldn't. The defeated look on her face nearly did him in, but his head stubbornly insisted it was for the best.

His heart was another story.

Before he could talk himself out of it, he decided it was time to get everything out in the open. If he didn't say it just right, he had no doubt she'd let him know. Figuring it was best to start out casual, he began slowly. "I mean it about the job. I couldn't pay you near what you're probably making at the bank, but you'd have complete control over what you do and how it gets done. There's a French word for it."

"Carte blanche?" she suggested, brow raised in a mocking gesture that made him laugh.

"That's the one." Seeing that he had her attention again, he leaned in to close the gap between their chairs. "I'm good with the hands-on stuff, not so much with the numbers and advertising. We make a great team."

That got him a slow, satisfied smile. "Yes, we do."

It was now or never, Paul recognized, and after a deep breath, he boldly charged ahead. "In more ways than one."

Her gaze sharpened, and she edged close enough that their arms were touching. "You mean, personally?"

Paul took the fact that she wasn't laughing as a good sign, and he nodded.

"I think so, too."

As he leaned in to kiss her, he caught the scent of the rose perfume she'd chosen this morning. Her lips curved into a soft smile, and it was all he could do not to haul her into his lap for a more thorough kiss. Instead, he settled for something more restrained, resting his forehead on hers with a sigh. "I'm really gonna miss you."

"And I'll miss you, but Dad's counting on me the same way your family's relying on you."

"Yeah, I know," he agreed glumly. Then inspiration struck, and he said, "Merton's halfway between here and Roanoke. When you're not too busy, we could meet there for dinner or something. Sound good?"

Mischief danced in those beautiful green eyes. "That depends. What did you have in mind?"

"Promise I'll behave."

"That's not what I heard," she teased, playfully shoving him away. "I've learned a lot about you from the girls on the reunion committee."

"Aw, they make half that stuff up."

"What about the other half?" He answered with a grin, and she shook her head at him. "You're terrible."

"But you like me anyway."

Suddenly, she was serious, and she rested a hand on his cheek. "I'm not sure why, but I do."

Those last two words grabbed his imagination, and he pictured them trading *I do*s in front of Pastor Griggs in his grandmother's garden. It startled him. He'd never even considered getting married, but something told him that if he made that leap with Chelsea, it would be the one and only time he'd ever do it.

Rattled by the track his thoughts were on, he thought it best if he got away from her before he ended up doing something that would freak them both out. Standing, he whistled for Boyd. "I'm gonna get started on sealing that garden bench for Lila. She wants to take it home with her after the picnic tomorrow, and it'll need time to dry."

The bloodhound loped up the steps, and Daisy dangled down from her perch on the back of Chelsea's chair to paw the top of his head. When the dog's wrinkly face broke into a canine grin, Chelsea ruffled the fur under his collar. "They're so cute together. I don't know what she'll do without him."

Her eyes locked with Paul's, and he watched them darken with a sadness that went far beyond her cat's affection for her big, goofy pal. In a way, Paul realized, he and Chelsea were like them, opposites in every way but somehow finding common ground. That unfamiliar sensation rolled through him again, stronger this time, and he fought to keep a handle on emotions that were threatening to overwhelm his good sense.

"Yeah, he's kinda gotten used to her messing with him all the time."

"Maybe we could bring them to those dinners you were talking about," she suggested quietly. "Y'know, so they don't forget each other."

The cautious suggestion brought to mind the timid girl he'd known in high school, who apparently still existed inside the confident, self-assured woman he'd come to know. The woman who was drawing him in, step by reluctant step. If he didn't veer off soon, it would be too late for both of them.

"Sure, we can do that," he agreed, edging toward the door. "If you need me, I'll be out back spraying that sealer on."

"Okay."

Although he was supposedly in a hurry, Paul's feet had other ideas, and he couldn't quite manage to walk away from her. While she gazed up at him, he felt the pull of her like a physical force that refused to let him go. Finally, he broke their connection and opened the door to go inside.

As he strolled through the lobby, everywhere he looked he saw the touches Chelsea had put on the decor to make the plain space more inviting. It had a welcoming country vibe to it, from the old photos to Gram's new calico curtains framing the windows. In the office, everything was antique and well used, but now her slick laptop looked right at home there.

Just like its owner, he thought morosely. How the uptown banker's daughter had managed to fit in here so seamlessly was beyond him, but she'd done that and more since they'd been thrown together to bring the mill back to life. Standing in the middle of what they'd accomplished, he told himself he'd get used to her being gone. It might take some time, but eventually he'd learn how to get along without her.

Unfortunately, running the business on his own would be the easy part.

Sitting patiently beside Paul, Boyd whimpered, his forehead pinched with concern. Paul suspected he looked pretty much the same right now, and he reached down to pet his faithful buddy. "Come on, boy. Let's get to work."

The dog padded on ahead of him into the workroom, where Paul grabbed a can of sealer and the sprayer. Carrying them outside, he went around the sealed top of the can with a screwdriver and popped it with a little more force than was strictly necessary. When the metal cover flew up in his face, he jumped back to avoid getting the toxic liquid in his eyes.

That toppled the can, and the sealer spilled all over the ground. While he scrambled to keep his boots out of the growing puddle, he stumbled over Lila's bench and went sprawling into a pile of wood shavings waiting to be bagged up for sale. As he landed in a cloud of dust, Boyd yelped and took off like a shot.

Paul figured staying in one place for a minute might put a stop to his bizarre run of klutziness, so he closed his eyes and tried to relax. When he heard someone chuckling, he pivoted his head to the side to find Jason staring at him.

Stretching out as if this were the most comfortable position he'd ever been in, Paul growled, "Go away."

Instead, his nuisance of a little brother ambled over and sat on a nearby stump. "It's a good thing you're not using the lathe this morning. You'd be minus a couple fingers."

"Unless you're gonna be helpful and fetch me a new can of sealer, get lost."

"Get your own sealer," he shot back with a laugh. Then, in a more serious tone, he said, "It's not like you to be so clumsy. What's going on?"

"I didn't sleep much last night, is all. I'll be fine."

"Really? When does Chelsea leave?"

"Sunday."

"Two days from now," he pressed, as if Paul needed the reminder. "How're you feeling about that?"

Paul had been asking himself the same thing. Something had changed between them after the reunion, and he'd relived that amazing kiss a million times. But she was still planning to go back to Roanoke, and he was staying here to do everything in his power to keep his family's business afloat. They both had obligations to keep, expectations to meet.

The misgivings she'd expressed about her job must've been a knee-jerk reaction to Theo's heavy-handedness, he reasoned. She was determined to take over her father's presidency someday, with all the fancy trappings—and rose bouquets—that came along with it. Paul couldn't imagine himself ever fitting into that world, so it was probably best to leave things as they were. This way they could both move on and have the kinds of lives they wanted.

Since he wasn't about to share any of that with Jason,

he threaded his hands behind his head and crossed his ankles in a careless pose. "I'm fine with it. She was never planning to stay, y'know."

"But you like having her here. Any moron with eyes can see that."

"Sure. She's super organized, and she makes this place run like a top."

Not to mention seeing her first thing wasn't a bad way to start his days. Beautiful and smart, she had a peculiar knack for aggravating and fascinating him at the same time. In his experience, women were either gorgeous or intelligent, but never both. Just one more thing that made her special, he recognized with a mental groan. He had to quit thinking that way, or he'd drive himself nuts.

"Whatever you say." Standing, Jason kicked Paul's boot and waited for him to look up. "You can try to fool yourself all you want, but you should know everyone else sees you've got it bad for Chelsea."

Recognizing the truth when he heard it, Paul relented with a sigh. "You think she does, too?"

He took a few seconds to consider that, then shook his head. "I think she's too busy pretending she's okay with leaving."

Paul sat up and slung an arm over his bent knee. "We're gonna try getting together for dinner once in a while."

"You could have dinner with her every night," Jason argued. "Why would you settle for anything less?"

"I've done the domestic thing, little brother," he said, shaking his head. "It never works."

"It never worked before," Jason insisted eagerly. "This is Chelsea you're talking about. She might've changed a lot over the years, but one thing's still the same. She finds a way to get what she wants."

But did she want to be with him? Paul asked himself. And if she took that chance, then changed her mind about him, what would he do? Instinct warned him that losing her would leave him nose-diving to a level he wasn't keen to explore.

"Trust me," he said as he dragged himself to his feet. "It's better to leave things the way they are."

"I hope you know what you're doing."

Clearly disappointed, Jason left him there and stalked away. Staring after him, Paul muttered, "Yeah, me, too."

"I love it!" Lila exclaimed when Chelsea showed her the bench Paul had made for her garden. Running veined hands over the curved back and arms, she beamed at him. "This is just how my old one looked. I didn't have any pictures to give you. How did you ever match it?"

Grinning, he tapped a finger against his temple. "I got a pretty good memory."

"I already made a set of cushions for it," she went on, patting his arm fondly. "You'll have to come by sometime and see it all put together."

Cocking his head, he gave her a mildly flirtatious look. "If that offer includes pie, you're on."

She laughed in obvious delight and headed off in search of her husband. Impressed with the way he'd so deftly handled the situation, Chelsea smiled at him. "That was really nice. You made her day."

"Just doing my job," he replied with a shrug. "Custom furniture, that's me."

She'd expected him to be on top of the world today, basking in the glory of Barrett's Mill Furniture's grand reopening. Instead, his demeanor struck her as melancholy, as if something else was on his mind, bringing him down.

When she realized he'd spoken to her and she hadn't heard a word of it, she cupped her ear. "Sorry, I didn't catch that."

"I said, you must be really happy with the turnout. I'd guess there's more than a hundred people here."

"It's wonderful, but they're not here because of me. They want to see what's going on at the mill, and with you."

A slow grin spread across his face, and she barely swallowed a feminine sigh of appreciation. No doubt about it, this guy had the kind of personality that sneaked under a girl's skin and was hard to shake off. Much more than charm, she couldn't quite put her finger on it, but she had a hunch she'd be comparing other men she met to Paul Barrett for a long time to come.

"So you don't think they're here to see what's up with us?" he asked, eyes twinkling in fun.

"Is there an us?" she drawled, batting her eyelashes in her best Scarlett O'Hara imitation. "I had no idea."

"You haven't checked your messages this morning, have you?"

Wanting to avoid distractions, she'd purposefully left her phone at the carriage house with the few things she hadn't already shipped back to Roanoke. "I didn't bring anything electronic with me today. Why?"

In reply, he took out his phone and tapped the screen to show her a message from Brenda. There was no text, just a picture of the two of them during their reunion dance. They were smiling at each other under the spotlight, and she had to admit they certainly *looked* like a couple enjoying a romantic evening. The problem was, they weren't. In her current state of confusion, Chelsea couldn't decide if that bothered her or not.

That thought led to another, more troubling one, and she groaned. "She probably sent this all over town."

"I'd imagine. Want me to tell her to stop?"

"No," Chelsea answered with a grimace. "It'll only make folks talk more. I'm leaving tomorrow, so it should all die down by lunchtime on Tuesday. I'm just sorry you have to deal with it after I'm gone."

The grin deepened into something more, and very quietly he said, "I don't mind."

His voice was so subdued she thought she'd misheard him. But the fondness glimmering in his eyes said otherwise. "You don't?"

"Not a bit. In fact, I really like this picture." To prove it, he fingered a couple of buttons, and it showed up on the main screen. "Nice, huh?"

"Very nice." She was about to say something more but caught sight of her father's car. When he got out, he was on the phone, and she noticed that he was dressed as if he were going into intense negotiations at some high-profile firm. Apparently, to him a custom Italian suit was appropriate picnic wear. Cautioning herself to remain upbeat, she said, "My father's here."

"You sound surprised."

"I am. Other than project-related emails, I haven't heard a thing from him since our run-in a couple of weeks ago. I wasn't sure he'd come."

Paul angled to look over his shoulder just as the passenger door opened and another guy in a fancy suit stepped out. "I take it that's Alex."

"Yes," she hissed in exasperation. Seeing him here

told her Paul's suggestion that he made her father nervous was bang on. "I supposed I should go say hello."

"Mind if I tag along?"

Tilting her head, she gave him a hard stare. "To greet my dad or to intimidate Alex?"

"I'm pretty coordinated. I can do both at once."

While Chelsea normally preferred to fight her own battles, this time she decided to take him up on his offer to back her up. Maybe Alex would assume what everyone in town did and finally accept that she wasn't interested in him. "Okay, but mind your manners."

That got her one of his infernal grins, and she couldn't help laughing. "You're hopeless, you know that?"

When they reached the car, Dad was finishing up his call. Like a faithful lapdog, Alex stood nearby, close enough to be within reach if needed but far enough away to avoid eavesdropping. At least, that was what he claimed. Chelsea suspected he heard a lot more than he should, which was one of the reasons she didn't trust him.

"Good morning, pretty lady." It was his usual greeting for her, but today the smile she'd always interpreted as friendly came across as a cool, polished expression at the opposite end of the spectrum from Paul's country-boy grin.

She couldn't believe it had taken her so long to see his true nature. "Alex. I didn't expect you here today."

"Good. I wanted to surprise you."

"I've been so busy, I forgot to call and thank you for the roses."

"I'm glad you liked them." He offered Paul a hand draped in a vintage watch worth more than the mill's operating expenses for an entire fiscal quarter. "Alex Gordon. You must be Paul Barrett."

"Must be," he agreed, shaking briefly before letting go. "So what brings you all the way out here?"

"Theo told me Chelsea was doing great things with this old place, and I wanted to see her handiwork for myself."

He gave Paul no credit at all, she noted bitterly. It was as if she'd managed to drag the mill into the current century through the power of spreadsheets alone. If Paul hadn't been bristling next to her, she'd have hauled Alex aside and given him a piece of her mind. While the two men sized each other up, she realized it was up to her to keep this little powwow as civil as possible. "After you see the improvements, I'm confident you'll agree we had a great team working on the project."

Alex didn't respond, and his pale brown eyes were locked with Paul's darker ones in a battle of wills. She couldn't imagine why they were acting like a couple of possessive roosters, but she prayed they'd stop before things got ugly.

Thankfully, her father joined them and broke the tension by diverting their attention from each other to himself. After the obligatory handshaking, he said, "Good to see you again, Paul. This is quite a turnout you've got here."

"We're happy with it. Thanks for coming, sir."

"You sent an invitation, and I RSVP'd," he stated, glancing at his watch in an obvious hint that he was in a hurry as usual. "Alex and I have a meeting downstate early this afternoon. Could we get a quick tour before we go?"

"Sure. Follow me."

He fell in beside Paul, but to Chelsea's dismay, Alex hung back with her. As his steps slowed, it occurred to her that he was trying to herd her away from the crowd. While she wasn't thrilled with the prospect, she didn't know how to put an end to it without sounding rude, so she reluctantly went along.

When they were basically alone, he reached out and pulled her to a stop. "Could I have a minute?"

A glance ahead showed her Paul was talking to her father but keeping her within sight. That simple, protective gesture warmed her straight through, and she sent him a quick, reassuring smile. Before facing Alex, she dropped the grin and got serious. "Go ahead."

Apparently, he'd picked up on her exchange with Paul, because he moved to block her view of him. "Don't think I don't know what's going on here."

The accusing tone spiked her temper, and she snarled, "Oh, get a grip. We grew up together, and we're friends."

"That's not what Theo told me." Crossing his arms in a stern gesture that reminded her vividly of her father, he went on. "He said you never liked Barrett when you were kids, and he hardly knew you existed."

"Not that it's any of your business, but we're older now, and we've gotten to be good friends. Us working so well together helped bring this project in over expectations and under budget."

"I'm sure it did."

His insulting smirk was the last straw for Chelsea, and she decided it was pointless to continue this particular conversation. When she turned to walk away, though, he grabbed her arm and pulled her back toward him. "We're not finished."

She was so astonished by his manhandling of her, she didn't notice anyone approaching until Alex began to inexplicably back away. His stumbling motion alerted her that it wasn't his idea to move, but someone else's.

Someone large and incredibly strong, it turned out. She'd never heard footsteps approaching, but somehow Paul had sneaked up and put their unwelcome guest in some kind of wrestling hold. With him firmly in hand, the lumberjack-turned-businessman was making short work of forcibly persuading Alex back to the car.

"What's going on?" her father demanded as he hurried over. "What's Paul doing?"

"Something I should've done a long time ago. Not that way," she explained when he gave her a confused look. "But you need to stop encouraging Alex to pursue a relationship with me. I've never thought of him that way, and I never will."

"I had no idea," he confessed with a frown. "You're both so bright and ambitious, I thought you were a perfect match."

"Well, we're not," she said gently. "I should've told you that before, but you're so fond of him I wasn't sure how."

As he took in the tense scene outside his car, he astonished her with a rare chuckle. "Why do I have the feeling Paul has something to do with your ability to tell me now?"

The comment threw her, and she needed a moment before she trusted herself to speak normally. "I can't imagine where you got that idea."

"I see." Smiling, he kissed her forehead the way he used to when she was younger. "When you figure it out, I hope you'll let me know."

His uncharacteristically sentimental tone baffled her, but he didn't seem inclined to explain it, so she thought it best for everyone if he just took Alex and left. "Of course. Have a good meeting."

"I'm sure we will." When he neared the car, he called out, "Turn him loose, Paul. I need him in one piece."

Paul complied easily enough, and Alex eyed him with grudging respect before slipping into the luxury sedan. As her father shook hands with Paul, they traded one of those male looks she'd never quite understood. That it had passed between those two men in particular made her very uneasy.

All her life, she'd considered Dad a fair but stringent man. His sudden—and obvious—fondness for Paul had come out of the blue, and she wasn't sure what to make of it.

While he mingled with the crowd who'd come to see what was up at the old mill, Paul kept an eye on the lane winding in from the road. At breakfast that morning, Granddad had announced he was coming to the grand reopening.

"Of course we'll be there," he insisted. "Thanks to you and Chelsea, our prayers for the business have been answered. Where else would we be?"

For her part, Gram had quietly sipped her tea, but Paul couldn't miss the worry in her eyes. It told him she wasn't sure Will was strong enough to attend, and because of that, Paul wasn't, either. Every time a car emerged from the tree-shrouded road, he glanced over, hoping to see his grandparents. So far he hadn't, but he wasn't ready to give up just yet.

During a quiet moment, he glanced around to be sure no one could see him send a hopeful look upward. "You know how much it would mean to him to be here. If You could help make that happen, I'd really appreciate it."

There was no sign his request had gotten through, but in his experience, the Almighty didn't respond directly to anything. Grinning, he recalled his mother explaining God's timing to her impatient six-year-old son, who'd included a puppy in his bedtime prayers for weeks.

She hadn't told him to be more patient, just smiled and said, "Have faith, Paul. God does things His own way."

On Christmas morning, a floppy mutt of a dog had shown up, sporting a red bow and a collar with a tag that read Chummy. The best present ever, Paul remembered as his father's extended-cab pickup rumbled through the opening in the trees and pulled into the VIP spot he'd blocked off near the ramp he'd built over the side steps to the front porch.

Sending a grateful look heavenward, he did his best to appear cool as he sauntered over to greet their new visitors. Resting his arms on the frame of the open passenger window, he teased, "It's about time y'all got here. We're almost outta food, y'know."

"With Molly in charge?" Gram laughed. "I hardly think so."

"She changed clothes three times," Granddad complained from the backseat. "The way she was fussing, you'd've thought we were goin' to the White House to meet the president." Rattling the door handle, he grumbled, "Your father locked these doors on me. Get me outta here, would you?"

"I didn't want you bolting away from Diane before I had the wheelchair ready," Dad explained in a patient tone that told Paul he'd already done that a few times. "It's a big step, and you shouldn't be trying it on your own."

"Wheelchair," Granddad spat. "I hate that thing."

"If you don't use it, we're going straight home," Gram informed him in her sternest voice. "I came to enjoy the party, not worry myself sick about you tripping over something and landing yourself back in the hospital."

"What she said," Paul's mother chimed in, obviously to drive home the point that he was outnumbered.

Figuring he could end the debate in about five seconds, Paul reached into the truck bed for the offensive chair and hit the mechanism to open it. Setting it down, he dropped into the seat and pushed it back and forth with his feet. "Comfy. I've been here since six, and I'm beat. If you don't use it, I'm goin' to."

His grandfather blistered him with a long you-don't-fool-me look, then gave in with a sigh. "Fine. I'll use it, but I won't like it."

"You sound like me when Chelsea made me buy that stupid computer," he teased as she joined them. "Even made me learn how to do formulas and stuff."

"Which you're great at, of course. Just like everything else."

She added a fond smile, and he was reminded that after today, he wouldn't be seeing it anymore. Refusing to allow that to cloud this beautiful day, he grinned back. "I had a good teacher."

Their gazes met, and he caught something in her eyes he hadn't noticed before: regret. For the time they'd wasted fighting, for the fears that had kept them at a distance from each other until it was too late. He had a feeling she was seeing the same in him, and he looked away to keep the moment from dragging on too long.

Today was for celebrating, he reminded himself. He'd start missing her tomorrow.

With his usual excellent timing, Jason trotted over and greeted the new arrivals. "Glad you could make it, but you missed the fight."

"What fight?" Gram demanded.

"Some dude from the bank got rough with Chelsea, and Paul let him have it."

"Oh, it wasn't like that at all," she clarified with a chiding look for Jason. "I had a disagreement with one of my father's employees, and Paul walked him out."

Oblivious to her unspoken warning, he grinned. "Yeah, in a headlock. It was awesome."

"Don't you have a log-splitting demonstration to get back to?" Paul snarled.

"Taking a break."

"Break's over."

"Whatever you say, boss. He loves it when we call him that," Jason told them with a wink before strolling away.

"Actually, I hate it, but he insists on doing it anyway."

He'd intended the remark to lighten the grim look on his grandmother's face, but judging by the deepening lines around her mouth, he'd missed the mark.

"Did you really put one of your guests in a headlock?" she demanded.

"No, I used a double arm bar, and it did the job. Didn't even scratch the fancy gold watch he was wearing."

Granddad looked satisfied, but Gram shook her head in softhearted disapproval. "I thought you boys had learned to solve problems without getting physical."

"He tried to, Olivia," Chelsea said, "but Alex wouldn't listen to either of us. He started getting unruly, and it was time for him to leave. Paul didn't hurt him, I promise. Now, what would you like to see first?"

Gram hesitated, then apparently realized the matter

had been resolved long before she'd arrived, and there was no point in rehashing it now. Beaming, she linked arms with Chelsea. "Everything."

Looking like lifelong best friends, the two of them went ahead with his parents in tow. Paul muscled the wheelchair up the ramp onto the porch, and to his surprise, Granddad held up a hand for him to stop.

Concerned he might have overdone it, Paul asked, "Going too fast?"

"Just gimme a minute." Pausing, he looked over the yard and surrounding trees, then out toward the sparkling creek. Taking a deep breath, he twisted in his seat to look back at Paul. Gratitude shone in his eyes, and he murmured, "When I was lying in that hospital, I thought I'd never see this place up and running again, full of people like this. Thank you."

Those simple, heartfelt words sent a sudden rush of emotions crashing over Paul, threatening to sweep him away. All along, he'd been doing this for his grandfather, the man who'd walked in the woods with him, teaching him how to identify different species and what they were best used for. The one who'd given him his first pocketknife and praised his early whittling efforts, even when no one could tell what he'd meant to carve.

Today the resurrected mill held a special significance for Paul. He'd succeeded in time for Granddad to share in what he'd accomplished. Even cancer wasn't strong enough to conquer his spirit, but every time Paul looked, a little more of him had slipped away. He knew he'd done everything in his power to make his grandfather's last few months as happy as possible, but he wasn't ready to let him go just yet.

Fighting to keep those intense feelings at bay, he forced a smile. "You're welcome. Ready to go inside?"

"I guess we better. Hank tells me you've messed up the works something awful, and I need to straighten things out."

Thanks to the grumpy foreman, they were both laughing when they entered the lobby. Admiring the new collection of photos in the seating area, Chelsea was jotting down notes while Gram gave her the history of each one.

When she noticed Paul, his grandmother said, "Don't my cushions and curtains look nice in here?"

"They sure do, and they're comfy besides. Fell asleep there just this morning."

She rewarded him with a delighted smile, and Paul's mind drifted back to when he'd scolded Chelsea for pestering Gram with a sewing project. He'd assumed more work was the last thing she needed, but Chelsea had known better. The smug look on her face told him her mind was moving along the same lines, and he decided to give her this one. "Okay, you were right."

"About what?" Gram asked while she handed Granddad a small plate of Molly's famous molasses cookies.

They were still staring at each other, and he felt himself being drawn into the depths of those incredible green eyes. He'd been fighting that pull since the day she'd shown up at the mill, and finally he'd lost his strength for it. Giving up with a wry grin, he replied, "Everything."

The corner of her mouth lifted in a subtle gesture of victory, and she arched one brow in the pose that used to drive him nuts. Now he realized it was part of the package that made her who she was. Along with the dazzling smiles, sharp wit and unpredictable temper. She was all those things, and so many more he couldn't even begin to count.

And she was leaving tomorrow. If only he'd started listening to his heart sooner, he would've known that somewhere along the way, he'd fallen hard for Chelsea Lynn Barnes. His equal in every conceivable way, she was nothing he'd ever wanted but everything he needed in his life. Caring and generous, she'd found her way back to the faith that was so important to them both, and he could easily imagine being happily married to her until the day they put him in the ground.

Sadly, he had only one thing to offer her: himself. And for the first time in his life, he didn't think that was enough.

Chapter Ten

"I wish you didn't have to go," Brenda all but sobbed after church the following morning. Wrapping Chelsea in a fierce hug, she withdrew to arm's length but held on tight. "We should've been friends all along, but I'm so glad we finally got to know each other. Don't be a stranger, okay?"

"I won't," she promised, her own eyes welling with unexpected tears.

It had been like that since she'd arrived and had gone on even through Pastor Griggs's touching sermon about people keeping absent loved ones close in their hearts. Everyone from the Donaldsons to the Harknesses had stopped to say goodbye, giving her wistful looks as they made their way to their seats.

There was no denying it, Chelsea thought as she walked out with Paul and his family. The kind, down-to-earth people in Barrett's Mill were going to miss her. It was a stark contrast to the coworkers and supposed friends she had in Roanoke. She'd been gone most of the summer, but none of them had contacted her. No phone calls or texts, not even an email beyond business-related questions.

Of course, she hadn't bothered to keep in touch with them, either. On the rare occasions she'd felt guilty for neglecting them, she'd told herself she needed to focus on the task her father had set for her. The truth was, she'd been so happily occupied out here in the Blue Ridge valley, she hadn't given her real life a second thought. Now that she was on her way back to it—and not all that anxious to get there—she was wondering if her temporary amnesia meant something.

Shaking off the thought, she dragged herself back to the present as they pulled into Will and Olivia's driveway. "I'm sorry Will's not feeling well. Was yesterday too much for him?"

"Yeah, but he'll never admit it," Paul replied in a fond tone. "Gram's pretty beat, too, but they asked me to bring you by before you leave."

They'd been so wonderful to her, Chelsea dreaded saying goodbye to them. Considering his rapidly deteriorating health, she knew it might be the last time she saw Will. The realization made her want to weep, but she forced a smile. "Not a problem."

Paul offered his hand to help her down from the cab, stopping to stare at their joined hands. He looked as though he wanted to say something, then seemed to change his mind. But he didn't release her, and Chelsea was surprised to find she didn't want him to.

Inside, Olivia was reading the newspaper to her dozing husband. When she saw them, she traded worried looks with Paul but in a chipper voice said, "Good morning, you two. How was church?"

"One of Pastor Griggs's best sermons," Chelsea answered. "He's planning to stop by later so you can hear it for yourself."

The sound of their voices roused Will, and he squinted over at them with a faint version of his usual welcoming smile. "I'm glad you came by so I could thank you again for your help restoring the mill. Paul says he couldn't have done it without you."

"We make a good team," she agreed.

"I told Paul you would," Olivia boasted with a quiet laugh. "He didn't believe me then, but I think he does now."

Her grandson groaned. "Go ahead. Rub it in."

Since they obviously weren't feeling 100 percent, Chelsea decided it was best to keep the farewells short. Olivia embraced her warmly, just long enough to set Chelsea's emotions bubbling near the surface again. After promising to keep in touch, she retreated back to the relative safety of Paul's truck. He didn't say anything as he drove to the Donaldsons', and she appreciated him giving her time to regain her composure. Ten years ago, she'd happily left Barrett's Mill in her rearview mirror. Today it was the last thing she wanted to do.

When they reached the carriage house, something wasn't right. It took her a minute to determine what it was, but when she did, she turned to him with a sigh. "Paul, where's my car?"

"Someone must've jacked it while we were at church. And on a Sunday, too. What's this world coming to?" He scowled, but the glimmer in his eyes gave him away.

"All my stuff is packed in there," she reminded him, although he knew that perfectly well.

Continuing the charade, he pulled his phone from his pocket. "Guess we better call the sheriff. Course, with it being Sunday and all, it might take someone a while to get here."

Shifting to face him, she rested a hand on his arm. "If you don't want me to go, just say so."

He paused a moment, then said, "I don't want you to go."

He looked down like a miserable little boy, and she couldn't help reaching a hand to his cheek. When he met her gaze, she gave him a smile that held all the things she felt for him. There were so many—respect, admiration, exasperation. But there was one that trumped them all. "I love you, Paul."

Joy flooded his features, and he gathered her into his arms for a long, delicious kiss. Into her ear, he murmured the most amazing words she'd ever heard. "I love you, too. I knew it after the reunion."

Astonished by his confession, she couldn't resist teasing him. "Why didn't you tell me?"

"I didn't know how," he said with a sheepish look.

"But you'll arrange for Fred to sneak off with my car to keep me in town? That makes no sense at all." Grasping his face in her hands, she gave it a gentle shake. "I… love…you. How hard is that?"

"For me, it's always been impossible. Until you."

The adoration shining in his eyes made her heart skip with joy. "You drive me crazy, you know that?"

"Back at ya."

"We're quite the pair, aren't we?"

Chuckling, he dropped a kiss on top of her head and rested his cheek in her hair. "Yeah, we are."

And there in the cab of his ratty old truck, Chelsea made the most important decision of her life. She wasn't going back to Roanoke—she was staying in Barrett's Mill.

With Paul.

Epilogue

"And I promise," Paul finished his personalized wedding vows, "to always listen to your ideas. No matter how kooky I think they are."

Their guests laughed, and Chelsea couldn't help smiling at the mischievous glint in his eyes. He'd winged his speech, of course, and it was perfect. She'd worked on hers for days, and while it was a touching tribute to the man who'd become her best friend, it wasn't anywhere near as good as his.

Then again, she thought as they sealed their vows with a long kiss, it didn't matter. They were a team now, until death did them part. These days, that was more than enough for her. Not that she'd ever tell him that, of course.

"Oh, I just love weddings," Brenda gushed to Chelsea while they posed for one of Molly's semicandid pictures of the bride and her very enthusiastic matron of honor. "Don't you?"

"Absolutely."

Especially since she'd traded her usual bridesmaid dress for a gorgeous white gown, she added silently. And because she knew Paul meant every word of his promise to respect her and her ideas. That was love, she now understood. Letting the other person be who they were, accepting every part of them, quirks and all.

When Molly moved on, Paul appeared behind Chelsea and slid his arms around her waist. Nosing aside her fingertip veil, he kissed her cheek. "Happy, Mrs. Barrett?"

Nodding, she leaned back into him and sighed. "You?"

"Very. Except I still think everyone's trying to figure out how a goof like me landed such a classy wife."

Laughing, she spun in his arms to face him. "And I'm sure they can't imagine how you can stand a control freak like me for more than ten minutes."

"Probably." She gasped, and he eased the teasing with a quick kiss. When he saw something in the distance, he laughed. "I think my aunt Gigi's got her eye on your dad. Hope you don't mind."

"She'd be great for him." A nurse wired with the sunniest disposition Chelsea had ever encountered, Gigi was just what her father needed in his life. "He works seven days a week and goes home to that empty town house of his every single night. That's no way to live."

"Speaking of which, what'd Hank and Lila hand you earlier?"

"Their wedding gift. Two months free at the carriage house, so we don't have to scramble to find a house right away."

"That works for me, since Jason's at Gram and Granddad's now," he approved. "You sure it's big enough for us to share? I mean, I've got Boyd and a duffel bag, so I'm good. But you have Daisy and all that girl stuff."

"My condo was furnished, so all I have are clothes."

"Yeah? How many pairs of shoes do you own?" She gave him a mock glare, and he laughed. "Tell you what.

You keep me on the straight and narrow, I'll make sure you have a little fun once in a while. How does that sound?"

"Challenging. And wonderful."

Smiling because she had no desire to stop, she kissed him as Will and Olivia came over to join them. Will had resigned himself to his new motorized wheelchair, learning to use it so the family could relax and enjoy their wedding.

With a daisy boutonniere pinned to the lapel of his navy suit, he beamed at them both. "I can't tell you how pleased we both are that you wanted to be married here."

"There's no prettier place in this whole town," Chelsea assured him. "We couldn't have done better if we tried."

Reaching for Olivia's hand, he squeezed it lightly before continuing. "I pray you'll have many happy years together, just the way we have."

Olivia was uncharacteristically quiet, and Chelsea noticed her chin trembling before she firmed it and said, "It was a beautiful ceremony. The perfect way to start your new life."

They hugged Paul and Chelsea before moving away to say hello to the other guests. Some of the happiness left Paul's eyes as he watched them go, and Chelsea put her arm around his back in a comforting gesture.

After a moment, he pulled his gaze away and focused on her. "I know it was tough to get things together so fast, but I really appreciate you agreeing to get married so soon. It means a lot to me to have Granddad here."

"And to me. I wouldn't have had it any other way."

Clouds descended over his features, and he murmured, "He won't be with us much longer."

"I know, but we'll enjoy every day we have. Starting with this one."

Some of the misery left his eyes, and he rested his temple against hers with a sigh. "Love you."

"Love you more."

"Aw, come on! We're married, and you're *still* competing with me?"

"Not a bit," she retorted with a coy smile. "I'm *way* out of your league."

"Can't argue with that."

He added a laugh, and she congratulated herself on lifting his spirits. Arm in arm, they mingled with their guests beneath branches draped with twinkle lights. Because, at least for today, this was all that mattered.

* * * * *

Dear Reader,

Welcome to Barrett's Mill!

As soon as this idea began spinning around in my head, I fell in love with the town and the fascinating people who live there. Ever since I was little, I've been curious about…well, pretty much everything. It turns out to be a good quality for a writer, and I learned a lot about banking and sawmills, two industries that seem to have very little in common with each other.

Just like Paul and Chelsea, who on first glance are as different as two people can be. When they take the time to get to know each other again, they discover that with a little effort, their unique talents dovetail quite nicely. Their dedication to their families—and ultimately each other—forms the backbone of a story about accepting life's twists and turns and making the most of every day.

If you'd like to stop by for a visit, you'll find me online at www.miaross.com, Facebook, Twitter and Goodreads. While you're there, send me a message in your favorite format. I'd love to hear from you!

Mia Ross

Questions for Discussion

1. This is a story about accepting the things life hands us and making the best of them. Describe a situation where you've done that and how it worked out for you.

2. Chelsea's mother abandoned her as a teenager, leaving her to be raised by her workaholic father. This greatly affected the way she viewed her career, and it became the way she defined herself. Is anyone you know like this? Is that person happy, or can you imagine how they might change?

3. The Barretts are very close, and Will's approaching death affects them all deeply but in different ways. Have you been in a similar situation? How did you handle it?

4. Paul has a special bond with his grandfather, and he doesn't think twice about putting his own life on hold to revive the sawmill. Do you have that sort of relationship with someone? What would you do for them if they asked you?

5. People around town remember Chelsea fondly, although she couldn't wait to leave Barrett's Mill after graduation. Are your own memories of high school good ones or were they better left behind? Over the years, have those old images changed or remained the same?

6. While working on the reunion, Chelsea makes friends with women she barely knew ten years earlier. If you've gone to your own reunion, did you chat with the same people you did in high school? Or did you find you now have more in common with other classmates?

7. Paul's faith is the foundation he's built his life on, but Chelsea fell out of touch with hers over the years. When they attend church together, she feels embraced by the congregation—and by God Himself. Do you think it's possible to regain lost faith simply by asking?

8. The animals in this story were rescued by Paul and Chelsea. Have you ever taken in a stray pet? If so, what made you decide to do it?

9. Chelsea's father assumes she and Alex Gordon are a good match because they seem to be so similar. Deep down, she and Paul are much more alike in spite of their obvious differences. Have you ever been judged solely on appearance? How did you handle the situation?

10. For Paul, restoring the sawmill meant repairing the waterwheel so it would operate the way it did when his grandfather was a boy. Do you have a similar reverence for the past? If so, what's your favorite historical site?

11. In addition to bringing tourists out to the mill, Paul's furniture company offers many former employees

the chance to do the work they love again. Can you think of someplace in your area that operates as this kind of hybrid business? What makes it successful?

12. Near the end of the book, Chelsea realizes the life she had without Paul no longer makes her happy. If you've experienced this kind of epiphany in your own life, what did you do about it?

COMING NEXT MONTH FROM
Love Inspired®

Available August 19, 2014

HER MONTANA TWINS
Big Sky Centennial • by Carolyne Aarsen

Handsome firefighter Brody Harcourt has always had a soft spot for Hannah Douglas. When they're thrown together in the midst of the town's centennial celebrations, can Brody convince the widowed mom of twins to give love another try?

HER HOMETOWN HERO
Caring Canines • by Margaret Daley

When an accident ends ballerina Kit Somers's dancing career, her future is uncertain. Former sweetheart Nate Sterling and his adorable poodle will show her she has lots of options—including becoming his bride!

SMALL-TOWN BILLIONAIRE
by Renee Andrews

Injured and stranded in a small Alabama town, billionaire Ryan Brooks falls for beautiful shop owner Maribeth Walton. But when her past comes to light, can their future survive this country girl's secrets?

THE DEPUTY'S NEW FAMILY
by Jenna Mindel

When sheriff's deputy Nicholas Grey enlists teacher Beth Ryken to tutor his seven-year-old son, she'll teach the single dad how to trust—and love again.

STRANDED WITH THE RANCHER
by Tina Radcliffe

A snowstorm maroons city girl Elizabeth Rogers at Daniel Gallagher's ranch. Soon she learns to adapt to the rancher's lifestyle, but will she lose her heart to this rugged single dad and his sweet daughter?

RESCUING THE TEXAN'S HEART
by Mindy Obenhaus

All work and no play is Cash Coble's motto—until he meets adventure-seeking Taryn Purcell. She'll rope this Texas businessman into swapping his cowboy boots for hiking shoes—and his spreadsheets for their happily-ever-after.

SPECIAL EXCERPT FROM

Don't miss a single book in the
***BIG SKY CENTENNIAL** miniseries!*
Here's a sneak peek at
HER MONTANA TWINS
by Carolyne Aarsen:

"They're so cute," Brody said.

"Who can't like kittens?" Hannah scooped up another one and held it close, rubbing her nose over the tiny head.

"I meant your kids are cute."

Hannah looked up at him, the kitten still cuddled against her face, appearing surprisingly childlike. Her features were relaxed and she didn't seem as tense as when he'd met her the first time. Her smile dived into his heart. "Well, you're talking to the wrong person about them. I think my kids are adorable, even when they've got chocolate pudding smeared all over their mouths."

He felt a gentle contentment easing into his soul and he wanted to touch her again. To connect with her.

Chrissy patted the kitten and then pushed it away, lurching to her feet.

"Chrissy. Gentle," Hannah admonished her.

"The kitten is fine," Brody said, rescuing the kitten as Chrissy tottered a moment, trying to get her balance on the bunched-up blanket. "Here you go," he said to the mother cat, laying her baby beside her.

Hannah also put her kitten back. She took a moment to stroke Loco's head as if assuring her, then picked up her son and swung him into her arms. "Thanks for taking Corey out

LIEXP0814

on the horse. I know I sounded...irrational, but my reaction was the result of a combination of factors. Ever since the twins were born, I've felt overly protective of them."

"I'm guessing much of that has to do with David's death."

"Partly. Losing David made me realize how fragile life is and, like I told your mother, it also made me feel more vulnerable."

"I wouldn't have done anything to hurt Corey." Brody felt he needed to assure her of that. "You can trust me."

Hannah looked over at him and then gave him a careful smile. "I know that."

Her quiet affirmation created an answering warmth and a faint hope.

Once again he held her gaze. Once again he wanted to touch her. To make a connection beyond the eye contact they seemed to be indulging in over the past few days.

Will Hannah Douglas find love again with handsome rancher and firefighter Brody Harcourt?
Find out in
HER MONTANA TWINS
by Carolyne Aarsen,
available September 2014 from Love Inspired® Books.

LIEXP0814